Green Spirit Project

At EDGE Science Fiction and Fantasy Publishing, our carbon footprint is higher than we want it to be and we plan to do something about it. For every tree EDGE uses in printing our books, we are helping to plant new trees to reduce our carbon footprint so that the next generation can breathe clean air, keeping our planet and its inhabitants healthy.

THE
HOUNDS OF ASH
AND OTHER TALES OF FOOL WOLF

BY
GREG KEYES

EDGE SCIENCE FICTION AND FANTASY PUBLISHING

AN IMPRINT OF HADES PUBLICATIONS, INC.

CALGARY

EDGE

Edge Science Fiction and Fantasy Publishing
An Imprint of Hades Publications Inc.
P.O. Box 1714, Calgary, Alberta, T2P 2L7, Canada

In house editing by Richard Janzen
Interior design by Brian Hades
Cover Illustration by Julie Dillon

EDGE Science Fiction and Fantasy Publishing and Hades Publications, Inc.
acknowledges the ongoing support of the Canada Council for the Arts and the
Alberta Foundation for the Arts for our publishing programme.

Library and Archives Canada Cataloguing in Publication

Keyes, J. Gregory, 1963-
    The hounds of ash : and other tales of Fool Wolf / Greg
Keyes. -- 1st ed.

ISBN-13: 978-1-894063-09-8

    I. Title.

PS3561.E79H68 2008   813'.54   C2008-901582-7

FIRST EDITION
(i-20080306)
Printed in Canada
www.edgewebsite.com

Contents

Introduction

I was signing books in the University Bookstore in Seattle one evening when a fellow named Dave Gross walked up, opened a copy of my first novel The Waterborn to the map, and stabbed his finger down on a place labeled simply "giants".

"I want to know what's there," he told me.

At the time, Dave was the editor of Dragon magazine. The idea appealed and so I wrote "Wakes the Narrow Forest", and in doing so created Fool Wolf, a character who would wander all over – and off of – the Waterborn map.

Fans of vintage fantasy will see Fool Wolf's deeper origins in Elric, Dilvish, Conan, Cugel, and a host of other wonderful picaresque characters I grew up loving. They are also a nod across the void to a late friend of mine, and so hold a special place in my heart. Writing these stories was a real treat for me, and over the years fans of them have asked if they would ever be collected into a book. The answer – finally, happily – is yes. I'm delighted that Fool Wolf has found a second home at Edge. I hope you, reader, will be as well pleased.

Dedication

For "Hud" Ward Brandon Fry
The original wandering Mang

WAKES
THE NARROW
FOREST

Wakes the Narrow Forest

FOOL WOLF GLARED ANGRILY at the ghost of his father.

"Quit telling Yellowhammer what to do," he snapped, trying in vain to turn his horse's head back the way it had been pointed.

"Your mount knows his duty," the ghost replied. "He knows you were turning south. The giant country is north and east. You aren't much of a Mang, but you know that much."

Fool Wolf peered darkly at the cloudy apparition. It was still man-shaped but had lost its color. He could still see the intractable set of the old man's mouth, however, so well remembered from youth. Beneath him, Yellowhammer kept walking, ignoring the pressure on the reins, as stubborn as the old man.

Fool Wolf could be stubborn too. He swung his rangy body out of the saddle into the tall blond grass, walked alongside the horse long enough to extricate his sword, hatchet, and pack. Dropping them to earth, he plucked a straw to chew, lay on his back, and studied the graying sky.

"What are you doing?" the ghost demanded, voice like leather sliding on stone. Weaker than before.

"Resting."

"We have far to go yet."

"Tell me why you want me to go to the giant country," Fool Wolf demanded.

"Because I am your father, and it is your obligation."

Fool Wolf chewed the straw thoughtfully. "That cloud looks like a grass bear with a long neck, don't you think?"

1

The ghost was silent for a moment. "You spit on everything right," it muttered. "There isn't a camp anywhere that will welcome you — among all of the tribes your name is reviled."

Fool Wolf laughed. "I'm welcome enough, if not by chieftains, then by their daughters. I go where I want, I owe nothing, ask nothing. There is nothing I cannot have if I desire it."

"Because you have no honor. You are not a proper warrior, you deny your destiny as a gaan, and now you even refuse your own father his last wish."

"I don't wish to be a gaan," Fool Wolf said.

"It doesn't matter what you want," the ghost hissed. "The spirit chose you —"

"Old man, if you ever want my help, you will stop this talk right now. Not that I would ever forget what you did to me, but it's stupid to bring it up now."

"You still blame me? Your own laziness and cowardice —" he stopped, attenuated now to a thin smoke, and tremored. "I've come back to help you, son. Help you be Mang again."

"You have come back," Fool Wolf said, "because I got drunk and said your name, allowing your ghost to find me. You need something done in the giant country, something a ghost can't do, and I'm your only choice. Tell me what it is, or take Yellowhammer on and see if he can do it for you."

Again the ghost paused for a time. "So," he sighed at last. "It is good that I am dead, with a son like you. Very well. Give me something to smell — for I am weak — and I will tell you. But let me start with this; if you do this, you will be rid of me."

Fool Wolf sat up quickly. "You should have said that to begin with!" He rummaged through his pack, took out his bow drill, and started a small fire. He put a bundle of incense in the flames, pricked his finger and squeezed in four drops of blood. More reluctantly, he placed a small cup of persimmon wine where the fire would warm it.

The ghost leaned into the smoke, inhaling deeply, and color gradually filled him up. Now Fool Wolf could see the future of his own face — the same arched, narrow nose, sharp cheekbones and sensual lips — but withered with age. It irritated him.

"Not enough blood. The wine is sour," the ghost complained.

"I keep the good wine for the living. Tell me."

"A giant killed me."

"Too bad. That's what comes of going near giants."

"This giant is a very powerful gaan."

"So? Since your ghost roams free, he must not have gotten your name or your body."

"No. I flung myself into an abyss. I was lucky."

Fool Wolf snorted. "Yes, very lucky. You want me to avenge you, is that it?"

"No. I escaped, but he still has Slate Lightning."

"Oh." Fool Wolf said. The Mang and their mounts were relatives, descended in parallel lines from Nagemaa, the Horse Mother. Leaving Slate Lightning behind was like leaving a brother. Worse, it was told that the perfect mount and rider were often reborn together as one being, something every Mang longed for.

"Now you see why I need you," his father added.

"Yes. You need a good thief, and you raised the best."

"Stealing from one's enemies is honorable."

Fool Wolf laughed as he kicked out the fire. "Stealing gets me what I want, that's all. What I want is rid of you, so I'll steal Slate Lightning back. How many days ride?"

"Two months, if the weather is good."

Fool Wolf sighed, picked up his things, and remounted. "The weather won't be good," he said.

They crossed the great River Woman by walking on her, beneath glacier clouds and bitter sleet. A week later, Fool Wolf found a camp of people who did not know him, and so stayed with them a few days until they began to suspect his luck at the bones was not all luck. By that time he had an extra coat, two more horses, a new iron gorget, and some fond memories of a girl aptly named Chattering Laughter.

A month later, he crossed paths with a trade caravan headed to the warm, lazy towns of the south — Wun, Nyel, Glittering Nhol itself. Grumbling, he watched it vanish on the white horizon. He had meant to try his luck in Nhol that winter.

In all it took four months to reach the edge of the giant country, mostly through the territory of the Stone Leggings people, who attacked him twice. The first time, when there were six, he lost them in the hills. The second, when there were only two, he gained two more horses, four gold coins, another hatchet, food.

✝ ✝ ✝

He saw his first giant in the town of Ruwtya. It lay sprawled in the frozen mud of the street, thick black hair matted like a bison's, ice crusted, face hidden in huge hands. When they approached, it lifted a head too large even for its immense body. Its arms were longer than its legs, and its shoulders bunched like mountains. Fool Wolf figured it weighed about as much as a horse. Small, bloodshot eyes stared up at him from the caves of its skull as it fought — and failed — to stand.

"Drunk." his father's ghost said. "Most of the giants in Ruwtya are drunks, slaves, or mercenaries."

"That's what killed you?" Fool Wolf said, scornfully.

"The giants in the forests aren't like that," the ghost replied, and for once did not see the need to elaborate.

Ruwtya was not a big place, but it was busy. It was the northernmost point that the caravans ran to, where the cities of the south bought furs, mammoth ivory, iron, lumber. Home to no particular people, it was inhabited by traders from the Nholish empire, Stone Leggings who had given up the horse life and settled down, mountain tribesmen the color of fishbelly. The streets were narrow and fetid, all too often blocked by supine, prone, or staggering giants.

He found a stable for his horses and sold two of them for twice what they were worth, then went to the common house, a long hall ten paces wide but some eighty long, half buried in sod. Its three hissing firepits warmed his frozen bones, and the drink they served — an unfamiliar brew that tasted something like honey but more like smoke — was heady. Settled on a bench and watching a couple of men playing bones, he contemplated staying in Ruwtya for a while, despite the ghost's constant pestering. It seemed a place where things might come ones way.

He was admiring one such thing — hoping she would come his way — when a giant came instead.

It crossed the room like a dog, walking on its fists, massive head level with Fool Wolf's. At arm's length it stood, close-set eyes suddenly gazing down from the rafters. Muscles the size of his leg played across a chest as wide as the distance between a man's outstretched arms. It stank of damp fur, urine, and alcohol.

"You. Mang," It burred, in deep and reedy Mang.

"Yes."

"You come here to fight a Giant?"

"Possibly."

"I'm for you, then. That coat."

"What?"

The giant blinked slowly and tapped its chest. "You win, I dead. You get coat back. Get my skin too. You lose, you won't need. Good deal."

Fool Wolf blinked. Young Mang warriors sometimes came to prove themselves against giants, returning with tales of epic battles. Was this the truth behind their brave stories? Drunken giants hiring out as opponents? Probably.

"This coat will fit you?" He asked.

The giant poked at his garment, a finger as thick as a sword grip indicating the Nholish coins sewn all over it for decoration. "Coins fit my hand. Buy more wine. You ready?"

"Now?"

"Thirsty now."

Fool Wolf laughed. "I didn't come here for that."

"Why else? Mang come here only for that."

"Not this one. But maybe you can help me in another way, and thus earn something. I need a guide into the giant country. I'm looking for a particular giant."

The giant's eyes widened and he swayed. At first he seemed to be sneezing, but then Fool Wolf realized that the rheumy gasps were laughter. It leaned forward, fists on the table. "You go to fight Forest Giant? Elder?" He hooted a bit more, rapping the table with his knuckles. "Your name 'corpse,' then. That not who Mang fight, little man. Not smart Mang who want to live."

"I don't want to fight him. I just want to find him."

"We need no guide," a faint wavering above the candle flame interjected. "I know the way."

"You know the way to get killed," Fool Wolf answered irritably, wishing the ghost had stayed outside. "I want to live."

The giant looked a little confused by his exchange with the candle, so Fool Wolf added, louder, "we have a deal? You will guide me?"

"What giant you hunt?"

"I don't know his name. But the name of his territory is —" he struggled to say the word as his father had said it —"Uh-moko, or something like that."

The ridged brows arched, taking most of the high, sloping forehead with them, then collapsed back onto the small eyes like a mountain breaking. Without another word, the giant turned, dropped back onto its hands, and walked away.

+ + +

Fool Wolf paused in the birches, watching the hulking figure pull itself up the slope, dragging a sack behind him.

"You changed your mind," he called down, as the creature entered bowrange.

The giant raised it flat-nosed, pumpkin-jawed face to regard him.

"Yes."

"May I ask why?"

"No."

"I wonder how many arrows it will take to kill you, then? For all I know, you've just come to murder me and steal my coat."

The giant paused, then settled back against a tree, hairy paunch nearly hiding his squatting legs. He looked tired; understandable, given his weight and the steep grade. "Giant you hunt is my father."

"All the more reason for me to shoot you."

"You go to kill him. You won't kill him. But with your help, I might."

Fool Wolf turned toward where the ghost hovered, a smoke as pale as the birches. "I'm beginning to like this giant," he said.

The giant watched silently, sucking from a huge wine-skin, as Fool Wolf wakened the Fire Goddess with his bow drill and asked her to keep the night cold from stealing their lives. As branches popped in her yellow teeth, Fool Wolf rubbed his hands over the flames. "Do you know any of the local gods?" he asked the giant. "I should probably make an offering."

"Not know these here. Offer some fat."

"They don't like wine? Most gods like wine."

The giant cradled his wineskin as if it were an infant and wagged his head no. In the shuddering light, he looked something like a child, with his over-large head, largely hairless face and forehead, his round-eyed stare. A child, or a very old and hairy man.

Fool Wolf chuckled. "What do I call you, wine-skin giant?"

The giant nubbed its fingers against it brow for a moment. "Dog," he finally said. "Call me Dog."

"Dog, what do you have against your father, that you would cooperate with an enemy to kill him?"

"Mang not our enemies."

"We come and fight you."

The giant scratched his face. "We think you silly. Why anyone want to fight giant? But if win, more wine. If lose, die, maybe even better."

"Why?"

"If can't live in forest, stay drunk or die."

"Live in the forest then."

"Can't. Father live there."

Fool Wolf tossed more branches on the fire, and sparks swarmed skyward. "Somewhere else, then. Another forest."

"Nowhere else. Father has U'u'omqo, all its gods, ancestors, wives. The forest awake only for Father."

"But if you take his Uh-uh-mo — his territory from him?"

"Then U'u'omqo awake for me, ancestors and gods serve me. My older brothers all dead. I try to take territory once — I lose. Very hard to beat Elder when the U'u'omqo wakes for him."

"Ah," said Fool Wolf, starting to understand. "How big is your father's territory?"

"Take ten days to cross."

Fool Wolf nodded, thinking.

"Why you hate your father?" The giant asked, waving its knuckles at the ghost where it floated above the flame.

"You can see him?"

"Yes. He speak to me, too. Says you bad son."

Fool Wolf stirred the fire, silently.

"Yes, son, why do you hate me?" The ghost quavered.

Fool Wolf jabbed a brand angrily at the shade. "You should never have done what you did."

"I wanted you to be a great gaan — you wanted that too."

"I was ten! Of course I wanted that! You told me the stories of the great ones every day, of Snap Copper, who stole the Moon, of Zha Yazhbu, who fought the Meat Mother and ran off with her daughter. You filled my little-boy-head with all of that, and then took me t-to —" he stuttered off, poked angrily at the fire, and then looked back at the ghost. "You couldn't choose a reasonable totem for me. No, no. It had to be the most powerful god you

could find. I trusted you, and you didn't know what you
were doing."

"I wanted you to be powerful," his father said, paused,
and then, "The old ones said you could be the most powerful gaan in ten generations. I thought —" a peculiar
expression stole across the shadow face. "I'm sorry, my
son."

Fool Wolf felt his jaw drop. It was not something that
happened often to him. "Now there are some words I didn't
think you even had in your chest," he remarked, when he
recovered enough to move his lips.

"I am sorry," the ghost repeated.

"And I don't care." He stood up and turned his icy back
to the flame. Behind him, the ghost drew near his ear,
whispering.

"I tried to —" the old man wheezed off and started
again. "I know you are reluctant. I know you don't want
to call her from your mansion of bone. But you will have
to use she-who-dwells-in-you to defeat this giant. He is
too powerful for a mortal man."

Fool Wolf shook his head. "I have a plan already, so save
your advice." He turned back to the giant, grinned.

"Did we answer your question?" he asked.

"No," Dog replied, "But not matter."

"Don't worry, we'll beat your father."

Dog showed his chisel-like teeth, then gulped more
wine. "or die, this time," he said. "Almost as good."

✤ ✤ ✤

The land changed its mind often, in the next few weeks.
It was mossy heath and shattered rock, it was spruce and
Tamarack, it was frigid marsh. They crossed a snaking
granite ridge and Dog hung back, his eyes flicking about
like agitated bees.

"Here starts," he muttered. "U'u'omqo. Narrow Forest."

Below them, wind gods made love. Fool Wolf heard
them, rustling and moaning, singing through the bamboo,
pushing pale ripples across the swaying tips all the way
to the mountain-clouded horizon. It did not look narrow.

"How do we find him in there?" Fool Wolf asked.

The giant choked out his humorless laugh. "He find us. You have wine?"

"You drank the last a week ago."

Dog nodded sadly, blinked slowly, and started down the slope.

The cane spoke to them in a tongue of hushed rattles, enclosed them in a cage of a million bars. Within, the name the giant had given it made more sense. The dead shafts from the years before were thicker than his thigh and as tall as a splintpine, the new spring growth still mostly head-high shoots. The giant pulled up the young ones and ate them as they went along, somewhat defiantly. "Father's food," he would mumble, now and then. But Dog belonged here. Even Fool Wolf — who did not care — could see that. His charcoal-and-umber streaked fur was a shadow of cane, and he eased his suddenly graceful bulk through the forest with almost no sound, something Fool Wolf, Yellowhammer, and the other horses certainly could not do. He was a different creature from that pitiful thing in Ruwtya.

Toward sundown, they found a place where all of the cane had been tramped down, and the young shoots were gone. Despite Dog's protests, Fool Wolf elected to camp there, where he could at least see a little spot of sky. Fool Wolf took out his sword — fine steel, stolen from a Swamp Kingdoms mercenary — and began to sharpen it.

"Sword not help you against father," Dog opined. "Cut wrong way."

Fool Wolf kept whetting. "Maybe not. What do you plan to do?"

"Call him dead."

"That's quite a plan," Fool Wolf remarked. "I thought you might hit him or strangle him or something."

"Call not right word. No word in your language."

"Well, then. You said I could help. How?"

The giant munched on a bamboo shoot, mouth grinding like a cow's. "I never beat father if just him and me. While I call, you protect me. Distract father."

"That should be easy enough. I've been told I'm distracting."

He was more or less satisfied with his edge, so resheathed the weapon. He was about to ask Dog what he meant by 'cut wrong way' when he noticed something wrong.

Whippoorwills had been singing since sundown, but now their glissando lamentations were in unison, joined by the ululating shrieks of shrew owls, frogs, and thuttering bats. All the night beasts crying together, as if they were following the slow beat of a drum.

Or a heartbeat.

Fool Wolf scrambled to his feet, an instant or so before Dog.

"Search in your mansion of bone," his father hissed. "Release the goddess! Quickly. I could not defeat him, but you can."

Fool Wolf shot the old man a glance, and that was what he saw — not a pale shadow, but the old man himself, as he had been in the flesh, solid.

"We're under the Lake," he realized, aloud.

Dog scrunched his brow. "Lake?"

"The world is like a lake. We live above the surface, the gods and spirits below it. Gaans can travel beneath, to the otherworld, through the skins of their drums, but it isn't easy. The head of the drum is the surface of the lake, and beating makes ripples —" he trailed off, because Dog was nodding.

"Understand. Father need no drum. Where father walk, is all the same, below Lake, above it. Where father walk, always ripples. He walk, now. Forest awake."

As if to prove this, the bamboo rustled, as though swarming with locusts, and indeed, Fool Wolf felt hundreds of small things slapping into his face, arms and legs. When he caught one in his hands, it became a cool wisp of air. All around him, larger, more worrisome gods began crawling from their deep pools, burrowing out of the earth, climbing through the tops of the bamboo, singing as animals and Human Beings cannot sing. Eyes appeared at the clearing's edge, catching the fire and laughing it back at them. Slope shouldered canines, neither wolf nor dog, paced at the rim of vision.

Dog towered up on two legs, stretched his arms wide, and roared. Roar was actually not the right word — it was more like some sky filling trumpet, sonorous, brassy. He did it again.

An answer came that swept his voice away like a cottonwood leaf in a tornado. Fool Wolf felt it in his marrow, as each pair of eyes, each invisible god answered, and a giant stood up at the edge clearing that made Dog look like a pup. One Fool Wolf standing on the shoulders of another might be able to look him in the eye. His tree-trunk arms stretched up into the cave of night as if to pull down the sky. The gods, ghosts, and beasts fell silent, gathered behind him like obedient children. All, that is, save one, a stallion, coal black with ashy strips on his hindquarters, staggering toward them as if through a high wind.

"Slate Lightning!" His father groaned.

Dog trembled, but he inched forward, dropping to all fours and then raising up again repeatedly, a dance. "Now, Mang," he said.

"Wait!" Fool Wolf shouted. "Can you understand me?" He spoke to the greater giant, head thrown back, fists on his hips.

"I can." A Human woman said, stepping from the shadows. She looked Mang, perhaps twenty years in age. She might have been pretty once, before her nose and left ear were cut off.

"You cannot bargain with him," his father's ghost hissed. "You have nothing to bargain with."

"You can speak for him?" Fool Wolf asked the woman, ignoring the old man.

"He speaks through me."

"Good. Tell him I've brought him something, then. A ghost that once escaped him." he gestured at his father. "His true name is Sheshchugaa'en." He turned to his father. "Sorry," he said, "but now I'm rid of you — as you said I would be — and you and Slate Lightning are back together."

Dog and the ghost of his father both gaped at him. Then the big giant roared and his father jerked like a fish on the end of a sinew line.

"Son . . ." the ghost began, and then stopped, his mouth frozen in mid-word.

Dog let out a strangled cry of anguish. "You not help?"

Fool Wolf shrugged. "Sorry," he repeated, striding toward Yellowhammer.

Dog's whole frame slumped; Fool Wolf thought he would become a puddle. But then he straightened, and something hard glinted in his eyes, before he turned toward the larger giant and shouted again. For an instant, nothing happened, but then a portion of the beasts broke uncertainly from their pack and came to join him, crouching at his feet.

The elder giant roared and started toward Dog. Fool Wolf figured it was time to go. The whole forest shuddered with their calls, but everything seemed to be ignoring him. With his horses, he quietly left the clearing, picking his way through the dark bamboo. He could be out of it well before morning.

✠ ✠ ✠

Dawn came, a golden smoke drifting through his many-columned world. He was still in the bamboo, and the giants were still shouting at one another. Distance had not diminished the sound much, but had changed it. Their deep chested calls now sounded like drums booming in a deep cave. A horse-sized dragonfly with a body of molten sky whirred by, a wild god that was part boar and part bear crashed at the limit of vision. All night they had passed, latecomers to the brawl. Despite himself, Fool Wolf felt a bit proud of Dog for putting up such a good fight. He wished one of them would go ahead and die, though. The whole territory was sunken into the Lake, and he could not find his way out of it until the fight was over.

Midmorning, he noticed the tracks of a human being, probably a woman. That was intriguing — even if it was No-Nose — and so, having nothing better to do, he followed them. They shortly brought him up a small rise and a clearing, in which, to his surprise, sat a small yekt — a house in the style of the Mang, with log walls and a domed roof of bark. He rode near, cautiously.

After a moment, a woman came out. It was not No-Nose, but a shorter woman, perhaps thirty. Nice looking, from what he could see of her, though she wore a heavy bear cloak. Tantalizing bits of thigh peeked from it.

"Huzho, Shigiindeye," he called, the polite Mang greeting. The woman stared at him for a moment, frowning.

"Have you come to try and kill my husband?" she finally asked.

"The giant? You're his wife?"

"One of them."

"He has more than one?" This sounded better by the moment. "They all live here?"

"No. Each one has her own camp. Did you come here to fight him?"

"Not at all. I came to give him something. Are all of this giant's wives Human?"

She grinned crookedly. "Of course not. Most are giants. How do you think he sires children?"

"I was wondering that very thing," Fool Wolf remarked, dismounting.

"Stay there," the woman warned.

"I'll stay right here," Fool Wolf promised, holding up his hands. "As I was saying, I wasn't really able to picture — well, you know — though I was enjoying imagining part of it, if you know what I mean." He let his gaze travel a little obviously over her. "Anyway, I can't leave here until those two stop going at it, so I wondered — actually, could I step a little closer? This is straining my voice."

"A little."

"Good," he said, doing so. "And might you have anything to eat?"

"Stay out here," she said, turned and went into the yekt.

He walked over to the door. "I was wondering —"

"Stay outside."

"I'm still outside, as you can see. But I was wondering if I could just step in a little bit. I'm cold."

"A little," she said dubiously.

"I was thinking you must be lonely for Human men. Did the giant kidnap you?"

"No," she said, stirring something around in a cooking pot.

"Can I come a little closer, and smell what's in the pot?"

"A little," she allowed.

"I admire that cloak. Would you mind if I felt of it?"

✠ ✠ ✠

When they lay quiet on her sleeping mat, a bit later, the giants were still shouting in the distance.

"How long will it take?" Fool Wolf asked, tracing his hand over the slight brown curve of her belly.

"This is the longest of all his battles," she whispered, standing up and slipping back into her cloak. "I think you should leave now. If you're still here when my husband wins, it will go badly for you."

Fool Wolf was feeling generous. "Why don't you go with me?" he said. "I doubt he'll have the energy to chase us after shouting all night. I can protect you."

She looked at him in mild surprise. "I don't want to go," she said. "If I did, I would just go."

"I don't understand."

"It's good to be a Giant's wife. I do a few things for him — things Giants can't do very well. He doesn't ask much of me. I never have to sleep with him, because he doesn't care about that. I don't have to look after children."

"But you seemed to like what we just did."

She smiled and bent to kiss him on the forehead. "It was nice, and I'm glad you came by. You were gentle and thoughtful, which few men are. I've had bad luck with men. You were nice, despite your rude entrance —"

"I was in a hurry," Fool Wolf protested.

"I know. But your flaw is that you would never stay with me, am I right? And then I would be back in that world of men, alone."

"I might stay with you."

"No. I can sense something happened to you. You were in love, once. Did she spurn you?"

Fool Wolf drew a skin around himself, a bit chilly. "She died," he answered.

"You see? It's better I stay here."

"I saw a woman with no nose —"

"Yes. Giants are better husbands for us. Giants aren't cruel like that." She cocked her head. "How did she die, your love?"

Fool Wolf sought for his clothes. "I have to go," he said. "Thanks for your hospitality, and —" he stopped as, reaching for his leggings, he noticed a saddle-pack in the corner. It was Mang.

"What's this?" he asked.

"Something the last man through here left," she said. "He was after my husband, though he did not tell me so."

"How do you know?" He turned the pack in his hands. No mistake, it was his father's.

"He kept asking questions. Pretty sly, but I knew what he was getting at. Men aren't very smart when they aren't wearing clothes. He thought — he heard that the heart of an Elder Giant was a kind of medicine."

Fool Wolf cocked his head. "What sort of medicine?"

"To cleanse an unwanted god. For instance, if a gaan is host to an evil god rather than a helpful one."

"Ah," said Fool Wolf, breath catching in his throat. "Ah."

"Is something wrong?" she asked.

"Is it true? That about the heart?"

"No. Idiots get killed here every year trying to find out, but the answer is no."

Fool Wolf shook his head and knocked his fist against his forehead. "So stupid . . ." he muttered.

"Is something wrong?"

"No," Fool Wolf said, tiredly. "I just hate my father, that's all."

He went outside, checked his weapons, mounted Yellowhammer, and rode back toward the shouting. One of the giants sounded very weak now, and it was probably the wrong one.

✣ ✣ ✣

He found them in the same clearing, though it was much larger, now, the bamboo burnt, blasted, twisted from the ground. Dog was still trying to stand upright, having a hard time of it. His fur was pasted to him with blood and sweat. A few small gods and beasts still hung near him, but more lay piled dead at his feet.

The larger giant didn't look tired, nor did the legion swarming around him. In the daylight he was even more impressive than at night, his body shivering like a plucked lyre string, humming with power.

Fool Wolf didn't waste any time. He wheeled Yellowhammer around the edge of the clearing, arrows whining from his bow. The first three sprouted in a neat cluster on the giant's chest, and were the last to hit. He shot four more, all true, but none reached its target, deflected by a shield of boiling air. But blood started from the wounds — that was a hopeful sign. He pulled his sword, as the giant followed him with impassive eyes. It shuddered, growled, and spit.

It didn't feel as if three separate things hit Fool Wolf. The blow that knocked him off of Yellowhammer was like a hand the size of himself slapping him. But as he sat up, dazed on the ground, he counted three bloody holes in his own chest. That was not hopeful at all. Cut wrong way. The bamboo blurred into green walls as his vision faded, but he noticed Dog making one last try, leaping physically toward his father.

Well, that was stupid, he thought to himself.

Indeed. You need me, now.

He shook his head. Had he slept? He was in a cave, low roofed, water dripping all around. Roots trailed down like the earth's hair. Beneath him was nothing, darkness, a few stars, but he wasn't falling.

In front of him was Chugaachik. She looked like a Dirk-Panther, black, eyes phosphorescent yellow.

"Where am I?" Fool Wolf asked the goddess.

"In your Bone Mansion, where you've kept me all these years," Chugaachik growled. "All I ever wanted to do was help you, love you. I came to you in good faith, and you keep me locked away."

"You'll stay here, too."

Chugaachik — now a great, black Jackal — laughed. "Oh, I think you'll change your mind. You are dying, you

see, and when you die, the giant will keep you with the
rest of his beasts, along with your father. Won't you like
that?"

"Darken your mouth," Fool Wolf said. "He'll have you,
too."

"All together, then. How charming. Or —" her grin split
around to her long, pointed ears and her tongue lolled out
" — or we could kill this stupid giant and be about our
business."

Fool Wolf looked at the monster. "Yes. But I don't care
for your business."

"Liar. It wasn't so bad, that one time, was it?" She was
the most beautiful woman he had ever seen, dusky, black
hair with just a hint of a curl in it, naked body retaining
something of the cat.

Fool Wolf stabbed a finger at her. "I'll be rid of you."

"Maybe one day. Not if you die now. Better choose."

Fool Wolf bit his lip until blood came, knowing she was
right. He closed his eyes, and willed open her dwelling.
"Let's go then," he snarled.

He opened his eyes as Dog fell. Fool Wolf leapt, a cat
made of lightning, a running flame. The big Giant saw him
coming at the last second, and then Fool Wolf was on him,
tearing through his spirit guardians, sinking claw and teeth
into giant flesh. The small gods fell away from them,
confused. The Giant, swinging his huge arms too slowly,
opened his mouth to Call.

Full Wolf tore his voice out, and most of his throat, too.

✛ ✛ ✛

He awoke, painted in blood. He was in the woman's
yekt, and she was outside, spread-eagle, lidless eyes set
sightless on the sun. Fool Wolf put his head down, and
for the first time in many years, he wept.

Don't be so pitiful, a voice in him said. It was fun, and
you know it.

"I won't call on you again," Fool Wolf snarled. "Ever."

"You said that when we did those fun things with your
other sweet lover — what was her name?"

Fool Wolf clenched his jaw and forced the gates of his heart shut. He could do it, when she was sated, when it was too late. The voice faded, was silent, leaving him with only his own sobs.

A moment later, he heard footsteps and looked up to see Dog crossing the yard, limping and dragging one bloody arm. Behind him came a strange ghost, one with the body of a horse but the upper torso of a man joined to it where head and neck ought to be.

"The legends are true, then," he whispered.

"My son," the ghost said. "What have you done here?"

Dog, too, was staring at the woman's remains. "Why?" He croaked.

Fool Wolf put his head down. "You'll have to find new wives, Dog."

"All?"

He nodded slightly, then glanced up at the horse-man-ghost. "You see why I don't want to be a gaan, now, father?"

"I didn't know it was Chugaachik, I swear to you. I thought she was a different spirit, an ordinary lion goddess. She tricked me."

"Why didn't you tell me that before?"

"I never knew, until yesterday. A ghost can see what a foolish man cannot." His face twisted. "I never understood. You were right to give me to the giant. You should have left me with him."

"You never believed me. You always thought it was just because I was weak. Yet you came all of the way here and got killed trying to cure me."

The ghost looked away and shrugged.

Fool wolf wiped his face, got up, and started to gather his things, trying not to look at the woman or remember the others, the children.

"I won't be calling your name again," he said, very softly. "And I doubt that I'll ever roam the same plains as you. Be free."

"Thank you, my son."

"Go."

And the ghost went, like a candle winking out.

Dog was squatting on the ground. "Why you kill my wives?" he moaned.

Fool Wolf flicked him a weary glance. What excuse could he give that the giant would understand? None.

"It's better not to inherit too much from your father," he murmured.

He mounted Yellowhammer, leaving the Giant rocking there, and rode south. He would go the long way, past Ruwtya, and thence to the Swamp Kingdoms. That would take two or three months, four if he dallied. By then he should be ready for a drink, a game of bones, a little pleasure. By then he would be able to look another person in the face and smile.

The Skin Witch

THE TIP OF A DAGGER PRICKED into Fool Wolf's flesh, just below his ear.

"Times change, my friend," the lizard-eyed man across the table told him, matter-of-factly.

"I'm beginning to believe you," Fool Wolf replied.

"Good. That makes things simpler." The fellow blinked his squinty eyes languidly, and Fool Wolf revised his opinion — he looked more like an opossum than a lizard. "Now, I'm prepared to be lenient," the opossum went on. "If you haven't been to Nhol since the old days, I understand your expectations. It was catch-as-catch-can back then. Now it's more — organized."

"So you tell me." Fool Wolf toyed with the idea of killing the opossum. He could do it, and get the fellow with the knife behind him too, and probably everyone else in the stinking, crowded inn called the Crab Woman.

The problem was, that meant unleashing Chugaachik, and once that was done Fool Wolf couldn't control a thing he did for perhaps days. And the things he did when she rode his shoulders were always regrettable, even for him.

Besides, he needed information. Clearly much of what he remembered of the ancient city of Nhol was outdated. This fellow seemed to have more current knowledge.

"So what are the rules, now?" Fool Wolf asked, as courteously as he could with a dagger poised to penetrate his brain.

Opossum folded and unfolded his hands on the pitted wooden table. "The first rule is, you don't work without permission. If you want to cut purses, or run the

21

bone-game like you did today, you request a territory.
If we don't give you one, you don't work. If we do give
you one, you stay in it. The second rule is, you pay the tax.
Always pay the tax. The third rule is, when you hear
something, anything that might be important, you report
it to me. And then there's the fourth rule."

"Which is?"

"You don't want to break the fourth rule."

"Which is?"

The knife tip twisted. "Politeness and patience are
beautiful sisters. They are best seen together."

Fool Wolf gave a conceding nod.

"The fourth rule is, you don't take worm jobs, ever.
Those positions are already filled. If you take a worm job
— and in case you're stupid let me be clear that I mean a
hire to kill someone — then you'll meet someone that job
actually belongs to. Meet him, but never see him. Is that
all clear?"

"Yes."

"Good."

"And so, what now?"

"I'm the man who welcomes new people to town. I
decide who stays and who leaves. I like you, my friend.
I like what I've seen of your work. You play the wide-eyed
barbarian-in-the-city well, and therein lies your strength.
I'm going to take the tax you owe on your earnings — that
will be two soldiers. Then I'm going to take your initial
guild dues — that will be eight more."

"But I only have six soldiers."

"Not to worry. You can pay us back later."

"Thank you." Fool Wolf produced the soldiers and
pushed them across the table.

"No thanks needed," Opossum said, collecting the coins.
"Just doing my job. You may take the Eel Market as your
territory, for the time being. Do well and you'll get a better
spot."

The knife came away, and Opossum stood up, brushed
his silk robe, and nodded. Then he left the Crab Woman,
the three thugs that had been behind Fool Wolf following
him.

Fool Wolf watched them go, fingering the pricked place on his neck, wondering what the odds were of escaping the city before Opossum and his friends discovered that he had already broken the fourth rule.

✛ ✛ ✛

Well. Now we're in trouble, Chugaachik observed a little later, her voice a cat's tongue licking someplace inside Fool Wolf's ear. He smelled musk and blood, and his heart twitched, wrapped around dark, naked limbs and a hyena smile.

"Maybe not," Fool Wolf replied, finishing his wine. "After all, I didn't kill anyone, and I never intended to. I just took her money."

Pretty Lady. We could have had fun with her.

"Shut up."

Anyway, I'm sure that taking the money — even just the first half — is what's important. What will get you killed.

"Maybe."

Probably.

He left the inn warily.

The Crab Woman was on the docks, and even in the afternoon, it was a busy place. It always had been. Nhol was situated on the lower courses of the waterway simply known as "The River." It was the hub of a trade network that ran thousands of leagues in every direction, from the corrupt and distant southern cities of Lhe and Rumq Qaj to the dark forests and plains of the savage north, where his own people, the horse-loving Mang roamed.

Nhol had been through many changes in the past five years. From what he gathered, most of its nobility, never really sane, had abruptly crossed some threshold into total madness. The Emperor had ordered that the great temples dedicated to the all-powerful River god be ravaged and burnt to the ground. The priests had been stuffed into bags, beaten literally into pulp, and cast into the water. A number of monsters of uncertain but terrifying description had appeared in the river, slaying at will, and riots and fire had destroyed more than a fourth of the city.

Order of a sort had come two years ago, when Nhol was invaded by one of its own generals, Suh-something or other, backed by barbarian sellswords from the east. Soon afterward, the general apparently slipped on a marble floor and dashed his brains out. The present emperor was one of the barbarians, though he had taken the typically Nholish title of emperor, Chakunge.

But here at the docks, you would never know any of that had happened. Teak-brown rivermen in bright cotton kilts still swore, sang, sweated and drank. Whores in flimsy yellow shifts still flirted from upper rooms. Crowds of boys too young to sail ran underfoot, pretending to be pirates, and the stained boardwalks still smelled of tar, fish guts, singed meat, vomit, boiled lemons, cinnamon, and piss.

Fool Wolf wondered whether he could steal a boat without being noticed. Probably.

But he had just arrived in Nhol, after months of wandering and privation in the wilderlands of the Giants and Stone Leggings. He wasn't ready to give up quite yet. Besides, he had someone to see and a problem to solve.

Where are we going, Chugaachik asked.

"To get rid of you," Fool Wolf answered.

✢ ✢ ✢

The witch-woman picked at her dice with trembling hands. Her eyes were wild, and a thin drool of blood leaked from her left nostril.

"She is too powerful, this goddess inside of you," she rattled huskily. "Too wild. Even the sacred incense barely dulls her fury. Even knowing her name is of little help."

"You can do nothing?" Fool Wolf asked.

She laughed, bitterly. "When the River was still alive, he had many terrible children. Now wild things come into Nhol, spirits strange to me, and yet most of my knowledge is still useful when I deal with them. But this — thing — that inhabits you, this Chugaachik — she is like no spirit I have ever known."

"You must know someone who can help."

She took a shuddering breath and wiped the blood collecting at the tip of her chin. It smeared there, leaving a little red beard. "There might be one, an outlander like yourself. But he isn't easy to see. They call him Lepp Gaz."

Fool Wolf laughed.

"Why is that funny?"

"No reason," Fool Wolf said.

✚ ✚ ✚

Lepp Gaz had eyes of such pale blue that they appeared white. Fool Wolf had seen such eyes before, rarely, but in those cases hair and skin were similarly pale. Lepp Gaz, however, had dark auburn hair. While his complexion was light compared to Fool Wolf's copper-brown, it still had a healthy color.

"You told my servants that you had news concerning my welfare," Gaz said, speaking the language of Nhol in an accented but perfectly comprehensible manner. "What is it?"

Fool Wolf smiled slightly. "I don't doubt your generosity. But I come here at some risk to myself."

Lepp Gaz diffidently stroked the air with his hand, indicating the courtyard around them. It was a sumptuous place, furnished with stools of burnished teak, a hundred flickering lavender-scented candles, flagstones covered with the pelts of the fabled opal lions of Oell.

"You were hired to kill me. Is that what you came here to say? You need not fear me on that account."

Fool Wolf tried not to show his surprise, but he failed.

"Come. How do you imagine the lady She'de'ng found you? You don't imagine she's actually acquainted with your sort of man, or knows the places you might haunt?" His lips curved in amusement. "Here is what happened. Her servant found you in the Crab Woman and arranged a meeting. You met her on one of her husband's barges, where you were moved by her beauty and pathos — or perhaps just her money. There you agreed to murder me.

And now here you are! But what you don't know, I suppose, is that She'de'ng, poor dear, can have no secrets from me, and in fact, has accomplished my own purpose."

"That being?"

"Why, to bring you here, of your own free will, to my rooms."

"If you wanted me here, why didn't you just invite me?"

"Because if I had invited you, you would have been suspicious. You wouldn't have come. If I had tried to force the matter, on the streets, you would have resisted. You might have even summoned her, and that would have been — unfortunate. Here, however, my own power is very difficult to challenge."

Fool Wolf didn't care for the direction the conversation had taken. "I don't know what you're talking about," he lied.

"You are Fool Wolf, of the Mang, of the Broken Sky clan. You are a shaman, and your helping spirit is Chugaachik, a goddess a great power. She is a goddess I would very much like to have in my own possession."

"Ah, you are mad. Of course, I never intended to kill you. I came here because I heard you might be able to rid me of Chugaachik. If you want her, take her. If you can."

"I'm aware that you disdain her power, though why is beyond me. Still, this is a good thing. I desire her. You want to be rid of her. It's a perfect arrangement."

No, Chugaachik growled, I don't like this man. He doesn't smell right. We should go.

Fool Wolf hesitated for any eyeblink. Was the goddess afraid? She normally suggested evisceration, not flight.

Fool Wolf cleared his throat. "Again, why didn't you approach me with your proposition?" he asked Gaz.

"My reasons are as I stated them. Such is your nature that you would have feared a trick. I must also admit that it was a test — not of you, but of She'de'ng. I wondered just how badly she wants me dead. Now I know."

Fool Wolf remembered She'de'ng, the sorrow and hatred in her voice, the delicate, fine bones of her face. He was glad, in a way, that that part was real. He had never questioned her sincerity. He might have misjudged the situation, but he had not misjudged the woman.

"What happens now?" Fool Wolf asked.

"I want to study you, to divine the best way to extract her. Chugaachik is a dangerous goddess, and it will not be easy, even for me. I will require your presence in my sanctum for a short time each day. Otherwise, I think you will find my house — or, rather, the house of my archlord Kwer, whose favor I hold — very hospitable, and you may have your freedom in it."

"I can come and go?"

"It would be unwise for you to leave the house. It seems you've broken some rule or other of the local underworld and have a rather large price on your head. Within these walls I can protect you. Outside, I fear you might meet an untimely end."

"I wonder how they discovered I broke their law."

Lepp Gaz flashed a smile. "I think we understand each other, Fool Wolf, do we not?"

You don't understand him at all, Chugaachik whispered. Make no bargain with him. We can defeat assassins.

Fool Wolf shrugged. "I am loath to summon the goddess," he told Gaz, "but I will certainly do it to save my life. If I feel the need to leave this house, I won't fear backstickers."

"You should. You were in Nhol before the changes? You remember the Jik?"

"The priest-assassins?"

"Exactly. At times they killed creatures who wielded truly godlike power, and they did so with great success. They had weapons more potent than steel, I assure you. What do you suppose happened to the Jik when the priesthood was destroyed and outlawed?"

"Ah," Fool Wolf said. No wonder things had become more 'organized.' "Perhaps I will accept your hospitality, then."

"And my offer?"

"If you can rid me of Chugaachik without harming me in the process, I am at your disposal."

"It can be done, I'm certain of it." He motioned. "My servant will show you to your quarters. Don't hesitate to complain if you find them inadequate. I hope —"

At that moment, a man came bustling into the room. He was a rather rotund fellow, with chestnut hair and light skin. Six tough-looking guards in blue kilts followed close on his heels.

"Gaz, Gaz! You must do something!" the man said, waggling his thick fingers in agitation.

"What is the matter, archlord Kwer?" Lepp Gaz asked.

"She'de'eng! She's had another — eh — accident. You must see to her!"

"Of course, Lord," Gaz replied, smiling. "I'm sure it's nothing serious."

"No, surely not," Kwer said, a little uncertainly.

"Well, let's have a look, yes." He nodded at Fool Wolf. "My servant Padwuru will see to your needs. I will see you at dinner."

"A banquette!" the fat lord Kwer said. "To celebrate the health of my princess! For I know you could never fail me, Gaz."

"Your confidence is moving, archlord. A banquette it shall be."

☩ ☩ ☩

After a few hours alone in the sumptuous quarters provided for Fool Wolf, the elderly servant returned, bearing a silk robe embellished with crabs, eels, scorpion fish, and all other manner of river-creatures. After dressing in it, oiling his hair, and examining himself in the mirror, Fool Wolf allowed himself to be guided through corridors to a house adjoining Gaz's.

He was seated on a cushion at a long table furnished with a number of small dishes. Pickled catfish with strips of candied lime, salted almonds, turtle eggs stuffed with minced water scorpion, anise crayfish, black cheese fried with garlic, and twenty other things Fool Wolf couldn't begin to name.

Kwer sat at the head of the table, Gaz at the tail, and along its length some twenty men and women in rich clothing, most of the barbarian coloring.

Next to Kwer sat She'de'ng.

She was as beautiful as Fool Wolf remembered, clad in a loose robe of dark crimson swirling with black waves. That was open in front, and beneath she wore a gown of deep umber which clung tightly to her contours. Her hair was held up in a complex knot by a simple gold pin.

She looked sad and pale, and, when her gaze met his, betrayed. But she didn't look injured. Fool Wolf wondered what exactly the nature of her "accident" had been.

"To our emperor, my fathers, and all the clans of the Wurut," their host said, raising a cup of something called 'pzel' that smelled like pine resin. It tasted better than it smelled.

"And you, guest," Kwer went on, poking a bejeweled finger at fool Wolf. "From which of our territories do you hail?"

"Our friend Fool Wolf is Mang," Lepp Gaz said.

"Indeed?" Kwer said. "I thought they were never seen without their horses. Where are your horses, Mang?"

"I had some bad luck, not long ago," Fool Wolf replied.

"You must have! I've heard your horses are dearer to you than your wives. I've even heard that sometimes you take them as wives."

"Only when our choice of women is limited to Wurut captives," Fool Wolf replied.

Kwer reddened and his fingers gripped into fists, but then he relaxed and chuckled. "I suppose I can't protest, since as you can see my own wife is not of my people. But look at her! Who could resist such a jewel? Could you, Mang?"

"Only if she were the wife of my host," Fool Wolf replied, diplomatically.

"She was a princess, you know, the daughter of the old Nholish emperor. One of two, I'm told, but the other was killed years ago. So I have the only one, eh? The only real Nholish princess."

"Quite a find."

"A real Nholish princess and a Dzingar sorcerer! Perhaps I should add a Mang warrior to my collection, eh?"

Another course arrived: roasted pork with a sauce of mustard and black cherries, pigeons baked in paper, fried asps stuffed with black rice, heads still on, arranged on the plates as if preparing to strike.

"I love to listen to her talk," Kwer continued, stroking She'de'ng's silky hair. "The accent of the Waterborn is so charming. Say something, my jewel."

She'de'ng bent her head. "What should I say, archlord?" Her voice sounded husky.

"You see? You see?"

"Charming," Fool Wolf agreed.

"Sing something for us, nightingale."

"I can't, archlord."

"Of course you can. Sing for our guests."

She'de'ng blinked, then cleared her throat and began singing. Or trying to sing. Her voice rasped and cracked.

"What is this? Sing, I tell you!"

"My Lord . . . "

"If my archlord will remember," Lepp Gaz intervened, "The lady's accident?"

"What. Oh, yes. Quite right. Never mind, my dear, Please rest."

"Yes, archlord."

At that moment, a fellow in the blue batik kilt of one of Kwer's servants appeared.

"Archlord?" he bowed and knocked his head on the ground.

"What is it? We're eating."

"Someone has been captured in one of Lepp Gaz's traps."

Kwer clapped delightedly. "Just when I was in danger of growing bored! Bring him here."

"As you wish, archlord."

"And if he has any weapons, bring those, too."

"Oh, he has weapons, archlord."

✝ ✝ ✝

The man was Nholish and dressed all in black, and he did indeed have weapons — a sword, an assortment of knives, a garrote, a small blowgun with a number of wicked little darts. His arms were chained behind his back and his feet were hobbled.

"Oh, my," Kwer said. "Some sort of thief."

"An assassin, I would say," Lepp Gaz remarked.

"An assassin? Sent to kill me? What nonsense! I'm immortal." He looked at Gaz. "I am, aren't I? Your sorcery —"

"You are beyond harm, archlord," Gaz said, a hint of irritation in his voice.

The captive's eyes had focused on Fool Wolf, who suddenly had no doubt who the killer had come for.

The chained man said nothing, however.

"Well, you will talk, eventually," Kwer opined. "Gaz, would you entertain us, please?"

"As the archlord wishes," Gaz replied, rising from his seat. "Let him be unbound."

A moment later, the captive stood free. Though his face remained impassive, his stance suggested puzzlement.

"Your weapons are there," Gaz said. "I'll allow you a moment with them."

The killer hesitated for less than a breath. Then he was a blur, sweeping up his sword and knife. The knife he flicked at Gaz, but his course took him toward the guard at the door.

The knife missed Gaz by inches. He didn't flinch. Instead, he drew the slender sword at his side and pointed its tip at the assassin. He held it one-handed in a high guard.

The assassin's blade hummed a weird, shrill pitch and arced out, cutting the unfortunate door guard into two neat halves. The blade continued and struck through a foot of the stone wall with a sound like nails scratching slate.

He continued toward the door without pausing, but something unseen stopped him as abruptly as if he had run into a wall. The goddess in Fool Wolf's chest sometimes gave him glimpses of the world-under-the-world, where the force of spirit dwelled, but all he could see at the door was a faint wavering.

The assassin understood quickly. He turned and hurled himself at Kwer, perhaps hoping for a hostage. Gaz moved like a panther to intercept him, the first look resembling concern Fool Wolf had yet seen tightening his face. Kwer's bodyguards clumped around him, a wall of flesh.

Gaz and the assassin came together and their blades met, met again, then belled in a flurry of blows so elegant that the two men looked like they were fighting on a stage, not too win, but to entertain.

Fool Wolf blinked, and suddenly the blade Lepp Gaz held didn't look like a blade at all — it looked like a long, slender sting from some sort of insect, and Gaz wasn't holding it, it was part of his arm. Fool Wolf felt as if spiders were walking across his eyes. Shivering, he closed them, and when he opened them again the assassin was leaping high above a slash to his knee, counterattacking to Gaz's head. The downward stroke cut Gaz from the crown of his skull almost to his crotch.

At the same time, surely in a dying reflex, Gaz's blade came back up, and the assassin took two steps back, lacking his sword arm. The severed arm continued to hold the sword, which still lodged in Gaz, about where his belly-button would be.

Gaz drew the Nholish blade from himself with his left hand. "Interesting weapon," he murmured. Fool Wolf could see no sign that the sorcerer had been split in half. The cut had entirely vanished.

Gaz walked over to the stunned assassin and thrust his sword into his heart. Again, Fool Wolf had the illusion that it was a sting, or the greedy mouth of a spider, poisoning and eating all at once.

Bile rose in his throat, and the vision faded as Gaz sheathed the weapon.

"Oh, well done, Gaz!" Kwer cheered. "Most entertaining. The look on his face! Why it's still there, isn't it?"

It was indeed. The assassin, whoever he had been, looked as if he had seen the most amazing thing in the world. Perhaps he had.

"Thank you, Lord," Gaz said. "But if I may beg your indulgence, that was somewhat wearying. I should like to retire for the evening."

"Well —" a petulant tone crept into Kwer's voice. "If you must. Indeed, perhaps we should all retire. Nothing better is likely to happen tonight." He nudged his wife and winked broadly. "Well — maybe something almost as good," he chortled.

She'de'ng's face didn't change.

✠ ✠ ✠

Fool Wolf returned to his room as a very worried man, with several questions of a more than rhetorical sort.

The most important one was simple; could Gaz be trusted to remove Chugaachik from him without killing him?

Chugaachik answered that for him. *He will kill you if you let him.*

"Who is he? Why do you fear him?"

I don't fear him. But it would be prudent to leave.

"When have you ever been prudent, bitch-goddess?"

You should put aside your differences with me, for the time being. We are in danger.

"Differences? You tortured my cousin to death!"

We did that together, sweet.

"No. Shut up." He pressed her down where she couldn't speak to him. He couldn't hold her there forever, but for the moment he didn't need the distraction.

He went out his window, dropping to the stone courtyard below, in search of answers he could trust.

✠ ✠ ✠

Nholish palaces were inward looking, with myriad courts and no windows facing out. He padded silently from one enclosure to the next, remembering where Gaz's quarters were, hoping that there weren't any more assassins inside the walls. It wasn't long before he saw a lighted window on the second floor that seemed to be in the right place. He leapt and caught the broad casement and, with very little sound, pulled himself onto it. It was long and wide enough to lie flat on, and he did so to minimize the chances of being seen from below. Then he found a parting in the drapes and peered through.

He saw Lepp Gaz at once. The sorcerer was naked. Without his robes his body was hard and muscular, covered with tattoos of a singular blackness. He was holding his sword, standing as if meditating.

As Fool Wolf watched, Gaz placed the sword in his left hand and with a quick motion cut his right wrist. Blood drooled out, running black into a small cup. At first Fool Wolf thought the color a trick of the light, but after a few spurts it came out red. An instant after that, Gaz stopped bleeding. Then he signed to someone Fool Wolf couldn't see.

A man approached, a servant by the look of him. Gaz sat on a cushion in front of a low table. The man unrolled a bundle of thin needles set together in a round ivory base, so that they resembled a chisel. In the cloth was also a small hammer.

The man dipped the needles in the black blood, placed their clustered points against a tattoo-free section of Gaz's chest, and struck the base with the hammer.

Gaz howled, a strangling scream completely out of proportion to the amount of pain that should have been inflicted by a few small needles.

The tatooer moved the needles and struck again. Again Gaz gasped in pain, and his forehead was plastered in sweat, though the night was cool.

This went on for some time, until Gaz finally held up his hand to command a cessation. "Later," he gasped. "We'll finish this later. I want wine, now."

"Yes, lord Gaz," the servant said. He bowed and hurried off.

Fool Wolf watched for a few more moments, but Gaz just sat there. The half-finished tattoo was of a stick-figure man with a large, one-eyed head caught in the middle of a widening spiral. He had never seen the symbol before.

As quietly as a breeze across ice, Fool Wolf let himself back down into the courtyard. After reflecting for a moment, he found a quieter place and ascended to the roof. From there, Nhol was a vast, dark maze. No forest, no mountain pass was as dark as a city at night. The wan quarter moon made ashy plateaus of the highest rooftops, but around them was pitch. Beyond and below, the great River flowed, a pale and distant twin to the thick band of stars overhead his people called the trail of ghosts.

Chugaachik was back in his ear. Watch out, she said.

Fool Wolf dropped flat, just as something hissed by him, struck sparks against the roofing tile and whined off into the darkness.

Cursing silently under his breath, Fool Wolf slipped back down into the palace. How many assassins were out there? Could they see in the dark? The stories he remembered about the priest-killers of old Nhol made them to be barely human. He was starting to believe it.

And Lepp Gaz had killed one as easily as blowing his nose.

Fool Wolf returned to his room.

✠ ✠ ✠

He wasn't alone, he knew that almost instantly.

"Come out," he said.

She'de'ng stepped from the anteroom. She had changed into a sleeping gown of green silk, with a very high collar. She was very beautiful, and he felt the same stirring interest he had the first time he saw her.

"Ah," Fool Wolf said. "It's you."

"You lied to me," she accused.

"Yes," Fool Wolf replied. "But you didn't tell me everything, either. You still haven't. That Lepp Gaz is a sorcerer, for instance, or why exactly you want him dead. That fellow tonight, at banquette. That could have been me, princess." He cocked his head. "Why did you want me to kill Lepp Gaz?"

She stared at him a minute, her eyes sparking briefly with some unknown passion, then going dull again.

"We ruled this city, once," she said, absently trailing her hand along the bas-relief of a mudfish. "My family. The Waterborn. We were the children of the River, and none could stand against us. Power was our birthright. His waters flowed in our veins." She looked away. "Some were born with too much of Him and became monsters. My sister, Hezhi, was filled with such wild puissance she had to be executed. But those of us who didn't change, or go mad — we were destined to rule. I inherited very little real power. I did not care. I went to parties, I drank, I stupefied myself with n'deng dust. I was happy.

"Then it all blew away. They say the River left us, or perhaps even died. My father and most of my relatives went mad, and then the barbarians came, and killed them. I wish they had killed me. I wish I had been ugly. They kept my mother, too, for awhile, until they didn't like the looks of her. But that was before Lepp Gaz."

"Others have suffered more than you, princess. You could have done worse. Archlord Kwer seems to dote on you."

"Indeed," she said, very softly. "Do you think so?"

She unfastened her robe and let it fall, stood naked, chin held up proudly.

He saw now why she'd had difficulty singing. A crude series of sutures ran completely around her throat, looking very much as if her head had been cut off and then sewn back on. An ugly ridged scar circumscribed her arm just above the elbow. The rest of her body was pocked with scars from knife and sword wounds, burns, and abrasions.

"Lord Kwer loses his temper, at times," She'de'ng said. "Sometimes he does it for fun."

"Horse Mother," Fool Wolf swore.

"When he actually kills me, he calls for Lepp Gaz. Lepp Gaz repairs me so I can be broken again. And again. That is why I want Lepp Gaz dead."

Fool Wolf looked at her and realized his fingers were trembling, which struck him as odd. He had seen worse than this. He had done worse than this, when the goddess walked with his legs.

"I have a question, princess. Did Lepp Gaz ever stab you with his sword? The one he used tonight?"

"Yes. The first time my husband wounded me to death. I thought he was finishing me off. He stabbed me, and there was nothing. The next day I was awake, and alive."

"Put your robe back on," Fool Wolf said. "Put it back on and leave me."

"I want to die," she said. "I want to join my father."

"Leave."

She did, and Fool Wolf sat on the bed.

He looked back at the window. If he was fast enough, if he chose the right direction, he might get by the killers waiting outside. The odds were with him, really.

Call on me, the goddess suggested. I will get you out easily.

"No," he murmured. "I know what you would do."

And why shouldn't we? At this moment Gaz is weak. Kill him and take his sword. With that, we could do anything.

Fool Wolf coughed up a sick laugh. "Yes. How you would enjoy that. A harem of playthings you could torture to death and then return to life. No, I think I'll take my chances outside."

The goddess changed tactics. Gaz will know you spoke to her. He has her soul. He can see through her eyes.

"I managed that on my own, thank you," Fool Wolf grunted. "It doesn't matter. I can still beat him."

Don't be stupid. You have no idea who you are dealing with.

"Do you? Tell me then."

But the goddess fell silent.

✠ ✠ ✠

Gaz's regard felt like a flaying knife stripping off his skin. Fool Wolf bore it, trying not to flinch.

"She's beautiful, your goddess," the sorcerer said. He lifted a small cask and flipped it open. Inside was a vial of dark fluid. Gaz regarded it speculatively, then set the cask down, closing it.

"You can see her?" Fool Wolf asked.

"Yes. I have familiar spirits that allow me to see beneath the top of the world." He shook his head in genuine wonder. "Beautiful. She must be mine." He picked up a hollow bone incised with fluid characters and peered through it at Fool Wolf. "Yes," he murmured.

Kill him, now, Chugaachik hummed in his bones. Fool Wolf had a brief, violent image of sinking his teeth into Gaz's throat and tearing, of feeling blood tickle down his chin and chest. He shook it off.

"What will you do with her?"

"I've developed a new sort of sorcery," Gaz said. "A new way of collecting gods and using their powers. It really needn't concern you."

"How will you draw her forth?"

"I really haven't decided the best method yet. The trick is to keep her from manifesting in you during the process."

"That shouldn't be a problem. It's the one and only thing I control about her. If I will her to remain in my mansion of bone, she will."

The sorcerer smiled briefly. "Mansion of bone," he repeated. "Very poetic, you Mang." He rubbed his chin. "No, certain processes may allow her to free herself, whether you will it or not."

Fool Wolf nodded sagely, as if he understood. In a way he did. Gaz figured that if Fool Wolf believed he was about to lose his life, he would release her. Because he was pretty certain how the sorcerer intended to extract the goddess from his skin — with that sword of his. Lepp Gaz wasn't going to bother separating Fool Wolf's soul from Chugaachik's — he would simply take both.

Fool Wolf grinned. "I'll be glad to get rid of her. When do we start?"

"Tonight, I think. I need to review a book in the library at the palace, a treatise on related matters. Until tonight?"

"Of course."

Fool Wolf left the magician. As he was passing though the outer chambers, however, he heard a peculiar chanting

from behind a heavy door. The language sounded like
Nholish, but it resembled Mang, too. It might have been
an invocation, or a curse.

He walked past as if he hadn't heard it.

⊹ ⊹ ⊹

He pretended to lounge about the palace, eating, joking,
drinking, flirting with the women. But when he was certain
Gaz had gone off to the Royal Palace, he excused himself
to go to his room.

But he went, instead, to Lepp Gaz's suits. The outer door
was locked, but he had spent some time learning the secrets
of such civilized devices, and that youthful study paid off
now, as it had in the past.

The second door was locked too, and it took him a bit
longer to pick that, but it finally creaked open too, revealing
a second door made of iron bars. Beyond, in a small cell,
was the assassin that Gaz had bested the night before.

Alive. He glared at Fool Wolf through the bars.

"How are you feeling?" asked Fool Wolf. "The last I saw
of you, you didn't look so well."

"You are a dead man, Mang."

"You are a dead man. I saw you die. I saw that arm come
off. Yet here you are, and with both arms."

"You will never leave Nhol alive."

"Well, that may be. Right now I'm mostly concerned
with leaving this palace alive, and not in the state you are
in. We can help each other. Surely your grudge against Lepp
Gaz is greater than your grudge against me. Especially
when one considers that I did not actually violate your law.
I have not, in fact, attempted to kill Lepp Gaz."

The man cocked his head. "You have a point, though
the order for your death has been given and cannot be
rescinded. Still, I might be convinced to help you. My
brothers need never know. What do you have in mind?"

"Why are you still alive?"

The assassin considered that for a moment. "My life is
not in my body. It has been stolen but survives elsewhere.
Thus my body can be brought to a seeming of life."

"Correct. Lepp Gaz drew it from you with that sword of his, then had it tattooed onto himself."

"My soul is a tattoo?"

"So it would seem."

The killer ground his teeth silently for a moment, but then he took a long, slow breath. "A new kind of blood magic," he finally said. "Interesting." His eyes widened. "I struck Gaz, and he didn't die either. That means his soul is elsewhere, too."

"You cut him nearly in half. That means his soul probably isn't tattooed on his own body — he wasn't worried that you would hit it by chance. He let you cut him."

"Then where is his soul?"

Fool Wolf smiled. "There is a cask in his sanctum. In it is a crystal vial full of the same black fluid he extracts for his tattoos. That is where his soul is, I think."

"How do we get it?"

"Tonight, he is supposed to remove a certain goddess from my body. Never mind the details. I'll free you beforehand, and you will hide behind the curtains in his sanctum. When he begins, you attack him, and during the distraction I will open the box. I will signal you — the signal will be when I shout 'So!'"

"Why not the other way around? Why don't you distract him while I open the box?"

"Because I know where he keeps the key that opens the box, and will have it on my person."

The assassin glared, then nodded curtly.

Humming, Fool Wolf returned to his rooms. On his way there, he took a servant aside and sent a message to Lord Kwer. Then he took a nap, a grin stretching across his face as he fell asleep.

✠ ✠ ✠

Fool Wolf watched silently as Lepp Gaz took of his sword and outer robe and lay them on a table beside him. The sorcerer then lit several braziers and sprinkled various powders into them. Smoke puffed up, aromatic and spicy. She'de'ng, who sat behind the table, coughed and looked more puzzled than usual.

"You seem nervous," Lepp Gaz said to Fool Wolf, as he fussed around with his equipment. "I assure you, this will be both painless and harmless."

"I don't like sorcery, no matter how painless," Fool Wolf admitted.

"Understandable. Do you think you will miss her?"

"Would you miss boils on your genitals?"

"Her curse makes you very powerful."

"It also makes me very unpopular. You aren't trying to talk me out of this, are you?"

"Not at all."

"Why is the princess here?"

Gaz smiled at him. Then he walked, very near, so near his lips were nearly touching Fool Wolf's ear. "My darling Chugaachik will need a body. She'de'ng is both durable and attractive."

Fool Wolf felt an odd tingle on his scalp.

"What?" He managed.

"She will be my mate, your goddess. I have sought her for a long time."

Kill him. Kill him now, Chugaachik said.

You know him?

He isn't Human. Kill him. I promise you, once he is dead, I return your body. I swear it.

"She's talking to you, isn't she?" Gaz said. He kissed Fool Wolf on the side of the head. "Don't worry, my sweet. We will be together again, as once we were. As once we were." He straightened. "Now —" the door suddenly swung open, and Kwer stood there.

"Hah! Hello, Gaz," the archlord said. "Caught you!"

"Archlord?"

"She'de'ng. I know you've been seeing her. I —"

Everyone Fool Wolf wanted in the room was now here. "So!" he shouted, and leapt into motion.

Except that his legs failed him. They felt like dead snakes. The smoke, he realized suddenly.

Meanwhile, the assassin bounded from behind the curtains, leaping straight for the little cask on the table, rather than toward Gaz, as they had agreed. Lepp Gaz merely watched him, a sneer on his face.

When the man touched the box, the air barked and a purplish flash enveloped the assassin. He fell to the floor twitching. Gaz regarded him for a moment, then turned his gaze back to Fool Wolf, who was still struggling toward Kwer, now on hands and knees.

"Oh, very good, Wolf," the sorcerer said. "You never intended to go after the cask. You never thought my soul was there at all. You lied to our assassin friend, here."

"What is going on?" Kwer demanded.

"Our Mang friend has discovered a certain secret," Lepp Gaz said.

"He knows about you and She'de'ng, too?"

Lepp Gaz blinked and sighed. "No, you imbecile."

"Then why is she right —" the archlord goggled.

"What did you call me? She'de'ng, come here!"

She'de'ng moved toward her husband, her head down, arms straight at her sides. There was something odd about the right side of her dress, as if she had something hidden under it.

Gaz turned back to Fool Wolf. "How did you guess?"

"That your soul is tattooed on Kwer? Why else would you tolerate the fat fool, when you could so easily be his master? And he is an archlord, well fed, well protected. A safer place for a soul than in an egg on a far mountain guarded by lions, if the old stories are to be trusted."

"My tattoo?" Kwer said. "It makes me immortal. Gaz, doesn't it make me immortal?"

Gaz ignored Kwer. "You lied to the assassin because you know I can see through his eyes," Gaz said, nodding approval.

"Of course. As you can see through She'de'ng's — that's what you meant when you said she couldn't have secrets from you."

"But I can," She'de'ng said. Everyone turned to her in surprise. "Lepp Gaz can see what I see, but he can't know what I think, feel what I feel -- or see what I choose not to look at." She lifted her robe, and Kwer turned away from her, back toward Gaz and Fool Wolf, an expression of complete bafflement on his face.

"No!" Lepp Gaz suddenly snapped his wrist up in a series of complex signs, muttering an invocation. Then he made a peculiar sound, half gasp and half suck. Kwer made an altogether different peculiar sound, something like the high pitched, surprised shriek of a baby. He had cause, at least. The point of Lepp Gaz's peculiar sword was sticking out of his stomach, a handspan beneath where his belly button ought to be. The red blade waggled obscenely, then withdrew like a worm back into its hole. Kwer, looking frightened and offended, toppled forward.

She'de'ng withdrew the sword and held its bloody length before her.

"Give me that," Lepp Gaz demanded.

"Not yet," She'de'ng replied. "I wish to speak first. As you must know, I passed your sword not only through Kwer's fat belly, but through the odd tattoo on his lower back. Your soul is now in my blood, so I suggest you listen to me."

Gaz was looking very pale. "The sword won't work for you," he growled.

"I felt it work," She'de'ng replied, haughtiness creeping into her voice. "I am not ignorant to the ways of power, as you must know from having stolen mine. I am Waterborn."

Fool Wolf had managed to get dizzily to his feet. He leaned against the wall. "You planned all of this," he accused. "Me, the assassin — all distractions to give you just two breaths to pick up that sword and kill your husband."

She smiled. "Yes. It had to be this sword, and no other. Because now I have something Lepp Gaz desires, whereas with any other weapon I would only have a dead husband, one easily raised back to life."

"And what do you want now?" Gaz grunted.

"I want your soul on my skin," she told the sorcerer. "Then I know you will treat me well — that I will be safe." She kicked Kwer's unmoving corpse. "I want his soul, too, and him alive again, as many times as I want him to be. Give me those things, and you can have your sword back, and I will be your friend and ally."

Gaz seemed to consider that. "I've underestimated you," he said, finally. "And I'm impressed. I agree. My life will be safer with you than with that fool, anyway. What of the Mang?"

"I couldn't care less," She'de'ng replied, dismissivly.

"The Mang is leaving," Fool Wolf grunted. "Gaz, you haven't lifted a finger to take control of this situation. Because you can't. As long as your soul is locked up in her blood, you have no power."

"Oh, I have power."

"Not much, I think. If you try to stop me, I release Chugaachik. That you will not like at all. Princess, you will like it even less."

Do it! Chugaachik all but shrieked in his head. he had never heard her sound so — almost panicked. This may be our last chance!

"You're bluffing," Gaz said.

"No," Fool Wolf lied, "I'm not. You claim to know Chugaachik? Imagine her with that sword." He let that sink in, then repeated, "I'm leaving."

Gaz spoke almost gently. "I will find you," he said. "I have searched for Chugaachik for a thousand years. I will have her. I can wait a bit longer, but I will have her. Do you understand?"

Fool Wolf grinned tightly. "If the assassins outside kill me, you will have neither of us."

Gaz's face pinched, then relaxed into a smile. "Well done," he said, finally. "The moment is yours. You will regret this one day — very bitterly, I'm afraid — but I can see you're in no mood for that singular and important truth." He sighed. "There is an underground passage that will take you out. The brotherhood doesn't know of it. I'll have a servant show you where it is."

"Tell me where it is."

Gaz told him, and Fool Wolf left them there to consummate their new relationship. He took the assassin's sword and a knife, and with it persuaded four of Kwer's servants to proceed him in the tunnel, which was just where Gaz said it was. The first three succumbed to sorcerous traps

Gaz must have placed in the tunnel at some time in the past; the fourth walked with Fool Wolf into the night air of the desert outside of Nhol.

Fool Wolf stole a boat and turned it south. Chugaachik, oddly silent, did not trouble him, and by sunrise, he was in the Swamp Kingdoms, and ancient, corrupt Nhol a memory.

FALLEN

GOD

The Fallen God

FOOL WOLF AWOKE TO THE SOUNDS of blood dripping and a goddess laughing. The blood was his own.

So was the goddess.

His body had a numb, drugged feeling, but he wasn't in pain. He opened his eyes and saw himself reflected in a dark mirror. It wasn't a very good mirror, but from what he could make out, he didn't look well. His long black hair hung tangled, matted, and unbound, and of his face, only his thin, arched nose was visible. His eyes were the black hollows of a ghost.

Plunk! Another drop of his blood hit the mirror, and ripples ruined his reflection. Plunk. Plunk.

He was hanging, spread-eagle and face down over a pool of blood. Small holes had been cut in the veins of his wrists, ankles, and neck. They should have closed up, they were so small, but they hadn't, so his blood would well, bead like sap on a wounded tree, then fall.

Good Morning, his goddess said, still laughing.

Fool Wolf didn't answer, but instead knotted his muscles to pull at the wire that lashed him to the wooden board above. A broad strap supported him at the belly.

His muscles didn't cooperate very much.

That was a fine time we had last night. A fine time.

Fool Wolf remembered — or partly remembered — and shuddered. "Well" he muttered, "It looks like we're going to pay for it. Or I am, anyway. Good luck finding someone else stupid enough to be your host."

An impression of teeth, cat's eyes, the musky odor of a snake came and went with her return laughter. Nonsense.

All you need do is let me loose again. Those wires are nothing.

Fool Wolf closed his eyes. He remembered a girl and boy — how old? Fourteen, maybe. Twins. He remembered what the goddess had done to them, using his skin, his fingers, his . . .

"Oh, I don't think so," Fool Wolf said. "I'll manage on my own." The funny thing was, he couldn't remember how She had gotten loose.

When Fool Wolf was a boy, the shamans of his tribe — the gaan — had told his father that Fool Wolf would make a good shaman. To that end, his father had taken him on a search for a god to live in him, a spirit helper. It was the way it was usually done. Most gaans ended up with a weak, mildly useful god as the first guest in their "mansion of bone".

But Fool Wolf's father had aimed high, higher than anyone knew. And thus, through a prideful mistake, Fool Wolf had ended up with Chuugachik, not an ordinary goddess in any sense.

The nature of their relationship was simple. Chuugachik had vast power, but if Fool Wolf drew on it, he had to pay the price. The price was letting her use his body for a while, and he had quickly learned that such a price was unacceptable except when he had no other choice. So he kept her caged in his heart, locked up, and tried to ignore her when she cajoled him.

She had never gotten out before except when he called her. He could not remember calling her, this time. But he did remember — very vaguely — how it had ended.

"Someone stopped you last night," he said.

Absurd.

"No, I know you. You weren't finished. And then —" he couldn't remember. All he remembered was an old man with a beard, an irresistible command, oblivion.

"Ah. Awake at last."

Fool Wolf turned his head groggily. The pool was in a room made all of brick — ancient, yellowish brick that was so smooth and crumbly it almost resembled sandstone. It smelled like a charnel house. That was unsurprising, given the blood and the fact that the entire, dubious city of Rumq Qaj smelled that way.

The speaker was the old man from his memory. He looked as if he were carved from some very dark wood, but his long beard was whiter than ash. He was bald, but his head was tattooed with what might be some kind of writing. He wore bright robes of silk, mostly yellow and orange. "Do you remember me?" He asked. The language was that of Nhol, a city closer to Fool Wolf's faraway homeland. That was good — Fool Wolf could speak the local language, but not well.

"Yes, of course," he said.

"Good. And you understand why you are feeding the gods?"

"That part I'm a little unclear on," he admitted. "I wonder if you might let me down while we discuss it?"

Plunk, Plunk-plunk.

The old man walked closer. "No. Let's discuss it now." He smiled, revealing perfectly formed but yellow teeth. "My name is Haqul. I am the architect of this building you desecrated. It is my job to feed the Foundation, raise the towers — set things right when they are wrong."

Fool Wolf sighed. "What happened last night wasn't my fault. I —"

"You have a demon living in you. I rendered her quiescent."

Demon? The Nholish word actually meant "evil god", which had never made any sense to Fool Wolf. Gods weren't good or evil, they just were. Woodpecker gods were concerned about woodpeckers. Stream gods thought mostly about streams. Chuugachik was something like a cat, with a world of mice before her, though even he wasn't quite sure what she was a goddess of.

That's what he thought. What he said was, "Ah — then pardon me for asking, but if you understand that much, why am I being punished?"

The priest smiled again. "You aren't being punished. You are atoning. It's not the same thing. Your demon has no blood and so cannot atone, you see? You took blood from the Foundation. Now you give it back."

"The girl and boy?"

"Over the years they would have contributed much blood, helped keep the gutters of the Foundation wet. They were my grandchildren."

"I'm sorry. I didn't come here for that — I didn't come here to hurt anyone at all. I came to see if you could help me. Help me be rid of my — demon."

"Well, then you came to the right place. Once your blood is gone, she will be rid of you. Demons do not remain when blood lies quiet and dry."

"I was hoping for something that would leave me alive at the end."

"I might have done that, too. I might still."

Fool Wolf tried to keep his face neutral, but inside he felt a knot untie.

"What do you mean?"

"There are many ways to atone. This is one. I would like to suggest another."

"Does it involve me dying?"

"Not necessarily."

"Will I have to call on my goddess?"

"No. Would you like to hear the terms?"

Plunk.

"I don't have to. I accept."

Fool Wolf inhaled steam and a sharp scent that reminded him of crushed pine needles and orange skins. The bench was hot, the air was hot. He could barely breath. They had given him a wine that closed his tiny wounds, but maybe that was just a trick — maybe they intended to steam him to death.

Of course, the old man was in the darkened, sweaty room with him, his gaunt, naked body barely visible in the orange eye of the coals.

"You need to regain your strength," Haqul told him. This will help."

"Yes," Fool Wolf lied. "I feel stronger already. So — this other atonement."

"What do you know of our city?"

"That it's very old. That the gutters run with blood, day
and night. That you have powerful sorcerers here."

"Sorcerers?" He looked puzzled at the Nholish word,
for an instant, then his gaze sharpened. "You mean Tarumq.
Them-that-raise-buildings. Architects."

"If you say it, it must be so. Is that what you are?"

"Yes. I am the eldest and chief architect of this building. It is one of the tallest seven, and the most venerable."

"How impressive." He remembered the city, surrounded
by buildings so tall that no light touched the narrow streets,
that only moss and mold grew in them. Buildings like great
towers, with few windows. And he remembered entering
one, its passages like close, dark caverns, and wondering
how anyone could imagine living thus, much less doing
it. His own people lived on the vast plains and prairies of
Mangangan and Falling Sky, and even they seemed too
small at times.

But he still didn't remember why he had entered the
building,or how he had passed its massive bronze portals.

"When my ancestors came to this land," the old man
went on, "nothing had ever been built here. Not a hut, not
a single vault. We were called here to build."

"Called by the gods?"

Again that look of incomprehension followed by con-
descension. "Demons, you mean, such as infest your
barbaric lands? No — the buildings called us, the foundations."

Now it was Fool Wolf's turn to blink. "I see." He saw
all right. The old man had just said there weren't any
buildings when his folk arrived hadn't he? The old man
was insane. Wonderful.

"A building has spirit before it has substance," Haqul
went on. "It has a plan before it has structure. You must
know that. It was the buildings unbuilt that called us, made
us their divine instruments. And over the ages we have
perfected them, always building them taller, always coming
closer to the truth they would have us realize."

"How noble. What was it you needed me for, again?"

"A demon has invaded our building. We are powerless against him. We need another demon to fight him. You."

Fool Wolf weighed that quickly. Why argue with the insane?

"I'm your demon, then. Tell me where he is, and I will kill him."

"He is in the uppermost story, the newest, where the Foundation watches the stars. That's where you will find him."

"Well, I ought to get started then, shouldn't I?"

"In a little while. When you are purified, and your strength has returned. We can wait that long, to ensure your success."

✣ ✣ ✣

They fed him as if they were fattening a goat for slaughter, but they gave him only the weakest wine, never enough to get drunk. They did send him a woman, though, a pretty young thing, perhaps nineteen years of age. She didn't speak any language he knew, or if she did, she did not do so. The door to his chamber — a low, ugly room with no windows — remained locked.

After the second night with the woman, he grew bored with her. She didn't object to sex — in fact she initiated it — but she didn't seem enthusiastic about it, either, no matter what he tried. He started refusing her advances, and she spent most of her time in his room eating and sleeping.

After five days Haqul brought him his sword and his travel clothes.

"Follow the upward way," the architect said. "When you reach the sky, you will know you have come to where the demon is."

"And then?"

"When you are done, I will keep my bargain."

"I don't remember any bargain."

"The bargain is for freedom," the old man said. He motioned toward the door.

The stairways were damp and smelled of blood. He passed many rooms. In one, some sort of party was going one, perhaps thirty people eating and drinking, wearing masks that portrayed nothing he recognized. They fell silent when he passed them. He passed storage rooms and kitchens and sealed chambers, but after a time — a long time, it seemed — he passed empty rooms, and then rooms with occasional corpses, rotting untouched for at least two weeks if not longer. They looked like soldiers, or guards. There were many on the stairwell.

He didn't like the look of that. He went back to one of the empty stories and began searching for a window. After an hour or so, he found one.

It was narrow and high, and the wall it ventilated was thicker than he was tall but his whipcord body had no trouble easing through. The fresh air felt incredibly good in his lungs as he wriggled out onto the narrow ledge for a better view.

Outside it was twilight, the sky a sea of molten lead archipelagoed with floating islands of brass, copper, and gold. Against these hulked the other buildings of the city, cylinders of unreasonable bulk, black against the sky. The streets below — he guessed he could count twenty before he hit those slimy streets, should he fall — were already invisible save streams of tiny lights, flowing through the streets with their unseen bearers.

The ledge went nowhere, and the gray stone walls were almost but not quite sheer, tapering as they rose. He dug the tip of his knife into the brick and found it crumbly. He might be able to climb down using a burglar's steel claws, or knives affixed to hands and feet, but it didn't seem likely.

He went hunting through the storerooms and found, to his delight, several lengths of rope. He tested his weight on it by looping it through an ornately pierced and carved door lintel, and when he was satisfied it would hold him, starting knotting it together. He kept doing that until he had used all of the rope he could find, then returned to the window. He tied one end to a large cabinet — too large to fit through the window. Then, bracing the rope around himself, he approached the ledge again.

Now it was pitch dark outside. The clouds had thickened to hide the stars. That was a beautiful girl with a witch for a mother — no one would see his escape, but neither would he know how far he had to drop when he came to the end of the rope.

Well, he would take the girl for now and worry about the mother when he came to her. He set his foot on the ledge — and froze, gripped by the most terrible fear he had ever known in his life. It wasn't even like fear, no more than tinder is a volcano. It filled his belly as if he had been cut open and had ice shoved in where his entrails ought to be. It shattered every thought in him, every wish and feeling. His arms and legs quivered, and his breath came in shallow, retching gasps. He practically fell back into the room.

A few seconds later, he felt better. What was there to be afraid of? He had no fear of heights, he knew that for a fact. He started toward the window again.

Seconds later, he was back in the room, shivering.

It's an enchantment, His goddess told him.

I thought you protected me against things like that.

This one is too strong. I can help if you release me.

You lie, he replied.

If you say so. She purred, a black lioness with the eyes of a little girl.

Fool Wolf sat on the floor for a long time, thinking that this whole situation made no sense at all, trying to force the world to be reasonable. Then, cursing, he started up the stairs again.

✛ ✛ ✛

He passed another seven or eight landings, and noticed that something about the rooms had changed. For one thing, there were no more corpses — well, plenty on the landing, but none in the rooms. Instead, there were numerous small cells, linked together by low doorways. Each apartment had a table set with plates, a chair, and a large urn. The plates contained the dried remains of food, probably about as old as the corpses he had seen below. The whole section reminded him of a honeycomb.

He searched through a few of these, and in the third he visited found a bottle of half-drunk wine. It had started going to vinegar, but he drank a little anyway, as he puzzled at the small chambers.

He looked into one of the urns and blew the wine out of his nose and mouth, swearing. Red speckles appeared all over the polished white bones inside.

He ran back into the stairwell.

Ghosts. They kept rooms for their dead. He bounded up two flights, then slowed. If the ghost wanted to come after him, there wasn't much he could do about it. He should know — his own father had haunted him for months.

Oddly enough, after the initial worry passed, he felt a little comforted by the discovery. He was familiar with ghosts. His people offered them food and wine, just as they might a god. Like gods, ghosts could enjoy only the scent of the food, the vapor of the wine, but they still appreciated it. In this city without gods, it was the first familiar thing he had stumbled across. The fact that these people, too, were bound to offer their dead some solace gave him hope that he might understand what was going on in time to keep him from becoming a ghost himself.

Still, ghosts you were related to were one thing — the shades of dead strangers was entirely another, especially when you drank their wine and spit it on their bones.

He climbed another five stories through more of the same, until finally he came to a large, iron-bound door hanging loose on one of its hinges. He drew his sword and crept near, peering through.

"Come in," the demon said.

At least, Fool Wolf assumed it was a demon. Gods and ghosts he knew — he still wasn't sure what demons were.

The demon — if it was that — looked pretty much like a man. A tall, lanky man to be sure, dark-skinned like the people in these parts, but with hair the color of a timber elk's hide — a dark, rich red. He wore a sort of quilted outfit that Fool Wolf guessed was the underpadding for the armor he saw resting on a table nearby. He had curling designs tattooed above his eyes that made him look constantly surprised. He was sitting in the sill of a large window —

the largest Fool Wolf had seen in the building. Across his lap he held a two-edged sword half again as long as Fool Wolf's.

He looked tired, squinting at Fool Wolf in the light of an oil lamp. "You aren't a ghost," he said. He spoke the language of Lhe, a tongue Fool Wolf knew well.

"No, I'm not," Fool Wolf replied, cautiously, in the same tongue. He slapped his hand against the doorpost, to emphasis his materiality.

"Good. I'm tired of killing ghosts, the poor bloodless bastards." He hopped down and stretched his arm out. His sword was really large, larger even than Fool Wolf had first thought, and the fellow was holding it in one hand as one might hold a willow wand. "You aren't wearing armor, so I won't ask you to wait while I put mine on. Do you have anything to say before we fight? Rites to perform? Do you need to pray?"

"Are you the demon?"

The man uttered a sharp laugh. "They told you I was a demon? No, the only demon here is locked in that closet." He gestured toward a huge iron cabinet or vault. "But if the priests of the demon sent you, I'm sure it's me they want you to kill."

This was getting confusing. "The architects sent me. The ones who run this building."

"Yes, as I said, the priests." He peered at Fool Wolf again. "You aren't one of them. You look like a northerner."

"I'm Mang," Fool Wolf replied.

"Mang? That's at the other end of the world. You came a long way to fight me."

"I didn't come to fight you at all," Fool Wolf said, starting to feel irritated. "I came to Rumq Qaj for reasons of my own. These priests of yours captured me and told me if I came up here and killed you they would let me go."

"I wouldn't trust them. They are a foul, unnatural people."

"Well, we agree on that, at least. I would much prefer to leave, if you know a way."

"There's the window."

"I've tried that. The building won't let me leave."

"Really? How odd. Well, you may have to try to kill me then. Or — you could help me, and we could leave together. He placed the tip of his weapon on the ground. "I, bye the bye, am Uzhdon, the Opal of Nah, demon slayer. I have the sight, and can see you have a totem god in you. I do, as well — perhaps you can see him. He is the Seven-Bearded Hawk, the fourth lightning strike. May I ask your totem?"

"I prefer not to say," Fool Wolf replied, stepping a little farther into the room. "It's against my custom. Would you care to explain to me what's going on here?"

"It's simple. This place is an abomination to the world. The gods hate it. I have come to put an end to it."

"This place? You mean this building?"

"I mean the whole city. I'm just starting with this tower."

Fool Wolf found he had nothing much to say to that, at least not at first. It finally came to him, though.

"What?"

"This city, above all those in the world, is depraved. They bleed old people and little children to feed the dark magicks that keep their towers standing. They perform unspeakable rites —"

"What business is that of yours? You were born five hundred leagues from here."

"If you have to ask that, you can't understand," the man said, his brows drawing his tattoos into a dark mass.

"Let me try again. Exactly what are you doing in this tower? In what way are you bringing their depredations to an end?"

"Ah. I'm going to slay their demon, the one who holds the tower up."

"The one locked in the cabinet."

"Yes."

"So it locked itself in there, to hide from you?"

"On the contrary. The priests locked it in there. It was the demon who called me."

"To come here and slay it."

"Yes."

Fool Wolf rubbed his jaw. "Forgive another untutored question, if you will. If you do manage to kill this demon — and if, as you say, its magic holds this tower up — won't the tower fall, and you with it?"

Uzhdon, the Opal of Nah contemplated that for a moment. "I suppose it might," he admitted.

"You suppose it might."

"That's what I said."

"How do you intend to kill the demons of all of the other towers if you die destroying this one?"

"Oh — I won't die. My sword Hukop is a god, too, brother to my totem. While I bear him, I can't be harmed by falls and the like." He frowned. "Though I suppose it might take me a long time to dig out of the rubble."

"Then it's hardly fair for us to fight, is it?"

"Oh — no, if you best me in a fair match, Hukop will let me die. It's only if I am attacked by cowardice or by inequitable numbers that he unnaturally preserves my life. He is an even-minded god."

"Very well, then. Do you know any way to free me of the curse that keeps me in this tower?"

"No. Odd that your totem spirit didn't protect you. It looks — strong — to me."

If you fight him without me, he will kill you, Chuugachik whispered through his bones. And kill him you must. They will never release us, otherwise.

Fool Wolf shrugged. "I don't know why my totem failed, only that she did. So — you've been here for two weeks, and haven't been able to open the vault the demon is in. What makes you think you will ever get it open?"

"That's where I have a dilemma, right now," Uzhdon said, a tinge of regret in his voice. "I've been fasting and communing with my totems, and I do now know what will open it. Human blood. This whole tower is built on it. It's mixed into the bricks. It's the mortar and the solvent of all of their evil magic. And it will open that door, make the god fleshly enough to be slain."

"Well, the answer is simple, then. You need only let a little blood."

"Oh, I tried that," Uzhdon said, holding up his hand. A mass of scars covered his wrist like white caterpillars.

"Unfortunately, my totems take their task of protecting me very seriously. They would not allow me to bleed from a self-inflicted wound, not even a drop." He sighed wearily. "If only I had known this when I first stormed the place, it would be different. There was plenty of blood then. But after I reached this room, the priests stopped sending warriors after me. When I descend, hoping to be attacked, I find no one there. Once I went too far down and they almost trapped me, and I did get some blood then, but by the time I returned here, it was already too late — the blood was dead. It had no effect."

"How do you know this isn't just some fantasy of yours?"

"You have a totem — you understand."

Fool Wolf bit off telling the man that Chuugachik often lied to him.

"And that brings me to my dilemma. They must have been sure you would beat me when they sent you up here — they wouldn't risk supplying me with fresh blood. If they were so certain of you, you must be a hero of some renown, and I am thus loath to slay you. I am also loath to let you slay me, for that would prevent me from accomplishing my purpose, and I'm not certain — you will forgive me — that I can count on you to use my blood to release the demon and slay it should you kill me."

"I pity you your dilemma," Fool Wolf said. "If it would be of help, I will swear a solemn oath to do exactly as you ask after I've killed you."

"Truly?"

"Of course," he lied.

"And you would go to each tower in turn, and do the same?"

"Yes, I swear. You don't imagine I have any sympathy for these monsters, do you?"

The tattooed brow knitted again, and for a long moment, Fool Wolf actually thought the idiot would accept his offer.

"No," he said, finally, with great regret. "I cannot afford to be so trusting. I think we must fight."

"Very well," Fool Wolf said. "We shall fight, and whoever wins will use the blood of the other to release the demon and then kill it."

"You have a good nature and a noble heart, my friend."

"So I am often told," Fool Wolf replied. "Now — normally I wouldn't make much of this, you understand — but as you have a godsword and I have none, and as you have on underarmor and I have no armor at all would you consider taking off the last, so we can fight on more even terms?"

"Oh. Yes, certainly. If you will wait a moment."

Fool Wolf folded his arms and leaned against the doorframe. Uzhdon started wriggling out of the garment, though being careful to keep one hand on the pommel of his sword, Fool Wolf noticed.

As soon as the garment was shucked up around Uzhdon's head, Fool Wolf rushed quickly forward, wrapped his arms around Uzhdon's knees, and with a single heave, threw the Opal of Nah out the window. The hero gave a muffled yelp and was gone, his sword still clinging magically to his palm.

Fool Wolf looked down, but it was still dark outside, and the fear snatched at him again, so he quickly withdrew into the room.

After a bit of searching, he found a mound of supplies that the warrior must have scrounged from the lower rooms. Most of it was gone, but there was stale bread and pretty good cheese and some suspicious smelling sausages.

Sticking to the bread and cheese, he ate his fill and waited, ignoring the goddess snarling profanities inside him.

✛ ✛ ✛

He tried not to fall asleep — Chuugachik had more power in his dreams than she did when he was awake. If she was displeased, she could make his dreams exceedingly unpleasant. She could even draw him partway into her shadowy world, a place where even powerful shamans feared to go.

And so it was with some concern, several hours later, than he watched a filmy presence approach him in the lamplight.

It looked like an animal that had forgotten what it was. It crawled across the floor on misshapen legs, one of which looked something like a cat's, another limb more like a knobbed hoof, a third something like a turtle's scaled and clawed foot. There was no fourth. It's face was a bloated mass with lizard eyes. It looked at him dolefully, and he realized that he could see through it, as he might a ghost.

"Help me," it said.

"You are the god of this tower, I presume."

It snorted and shuffled uncertainly. "I remember . . ." it began, and then was silent for awhile, as if its words weren't a preface to a longer statement but a command to itself. But after a time it spoke again. He noted, with some interest, that it spoke Mang. "Long ago, I think. I lived here, but not here. I was something else. I remember things like columns, and things like gutters —"

"Trees? Rivers?"

"So you remember too?"

"I have seen them."

"Where?"

"Far from here. You used to be a Huugaada, didn't you?"

The thing made a sound he took for incomprehension.

"There are three sorts of gods," Fool Wolf said. "There are the Huugaada, who live in places — grove, a hill, the Mudune who live in things — like the goddess in my chest, or the god in Uzhdon's sword. Then there are the Yai, the gods of the mountain and sky, who made the world, but who are not often seen. You were a god of a place."

The god snuffled a bit. "People came, and they gave me blood. I liked it, and they gave more. They asked if they could build something to honor me, and I told them they could. After that —" it paused for a very long time —" So long. I miss what was. I want to die, now. I'm tired."

"That's a shame," Fool Wolf said. "But I think, soon enough, you may get your wish."

"Will you kill me?"

"No. This is just the shadow of you. The real you is all around me, and I can't get to you."

"The other said he knew a way."

"He does. Like I said, I don't think you have to wait much longer."

☩ ☩ ☩

It was around noon of the next day that Uzhdon burst back into the room, his huge sword in one hand and the bound, struggling form of Haqul gripped by the hair in the other.

"I salute you," Uzhdon said. "I should have thought of that a long time ago! You didn't have to push me, though — if you had only explained your plan, I would have seen the logic in it."

Fool Wolf grinned. "I couldn't be sure of that, though, could I? It's not natural to jump from this high, even if you know you will survive."

"Well — you do not know me as well as you might, so I forgive you. In any event, it was a perfect plan. They never expected me to come in through the front door again. Of course, at first all I could think about was getting revenge on you — that fall hurt, even if it didn't kill me. But then I realized what you were up to. They were all there, on the lower levels, and had nowhere to run but up! And look, I was actually able to capture the priest himself! Which is good for my conscience — I would have worried over killing a lackey or slave in cold blood, who might be associated with this evil through no choice of his own."

"Sacrifice?" Squeaked the architect.

"Quiet," Uzhdon said. "You have spilled enough innocent blood to fill a sea."

"But we almost never kill anyone," Haqul protested. "A living person can always make more blood — a dead one can make none at all."

"Even better — we may not have to kill even you to free the demon."

"You're going to free the Foundation?"

"Yes. So we can kill it."

"You're insane."

"It wants to die."

"What has that to do with anything? Do you kill each person you meet who expresses an interest in suicide?"

"This is different. This is an abomination."

Haqul looked straight at Fool Wolf. "You want to be free?" He asked. "Then stop this madman."

Fool Wolf understood, quite suddenly, that the priest was not talking to him. He was talking to Chuugachik. The priest then muttered something else, in a language Fool Wolf didn't understand.

But suddenly he felt his teeth ache to be sharper than razors, his fingers envious of talons, and thoughts like angry wasps filling his mind.

Now, Chuugachik shrieked, triumphantly. Now, now now!

And he remembered. This was how it had happened before. He had come to the city — to this building — seeking a sorcerer who could rid him of his terrible companion. And the sorcerer had set her free.

Only for a time, always just for a time, until she grew tired and sated with her horrible games.

He promised to make you ascendant if you tricked me. He promised to give you my body.

It's only what I deserve, sweet thing. I gave myself to you, to you alone of all men and women. Yet you spurn me, cheat me, deprive me. You could be the greatest Gaan, the greatest shaman who walks the earth today, who has walked it in four hundred years. Yet you refuse me!

The price is too high.

You lie. You love me. You love what we do together.

Fool Wolf remembered the little boy and girl, how their screams of pain had sounded like sweet music, had aroused him to the core. He remembered his first love, a cross-cousin from his father's family, how she had died without ever fully believing what her lover was doing to her. He remembered a woman he had spent a single night with, staked out in the sun to die, her eyelids cut away, and himself watching her, and humming a little tune.

He remembered the joyous feeling of power when the goddess had his body, his enemies breaking like Nholish glass beneath a hammer.

This priest can give us all of that, my sweet, forever. She was winning. He could feel his soul starting to swim to the little place he lived when she used his limbs. The architect was bringing her out.

The price is freedom. Not his freedom from the tower, or his freedom from Chuugachik — but her freedom to walk in his skin.

But if Haqul could do all of that, maybe he could take her out of him, as he had wanted in the first place.

She was winning. Soon they would be free, together, as it ought to be, and he could stop denying . . .

He was barely aware that he did it. Perhaps that's why she wasn't able to stop him, jerk his arm away. He did it on instinct, like a man finding his bed in the dark. His knife was in his hand and out if it, just like that, a silver fish in the air, a little tower standing out of Haqul's eye. The other eye stared wide, first at him, then through him, then nowhere.

Fool Wolf's heart snapped closed on the screaming goddess like the lid of a coffin, and her voice went out — for the moment.

He blinked. Uzhdon's blade was poised to split him in half.

"Why?" Uzhdon said.

"You have the sight. You saw."

"Yes. I saw him invoke your totem. It is —"

"It is contained," Fool Wolf gasped. "Use his blood while it is still alive."

Uzhdon hesitated for a few seconds, then nodded. Haqul's heart was still beating when the hero cut his throat and bled him onto the vault.

The blood boiled like smoke, and the vault began to creak open.

"We will talk when I am done with this," Uzhdon murmured. "That thing which dwells in you is fouler than anything that lives in this city."

"I know," Fool Wolf said. "I came here to be rid of her."

"She will have you one day. She must be stopped."

Fool Wolf glanced at Uzhdon, but the hero wasn't even looking at him. He was watching the misshapen god manifest and limp from the vault.

Fool Wolf threw him out the window again. It was harder, this time. The hero managed to spin and get off a vicious slash with his sword, and he was hideously strong. Fool Wolf watched a forelock of his own hair follow Uzhdon toward the distant street. That close.

"Kill me," said the pathetic little god behind him.

"No," Fool Wolf said.

"Please."

"No. What's the point? You're free now. Do what you want. They built this prison of yours out of your own will and their blood. It's yours to tear down if you want. But I won't help. It isn't my business."

With that he turned and made his way quickly down to the level where he had left the rope.

He felt sick again when he approached the window, so he cracked his heart a bit, so he could speak to Chuugachik.

"You can stop it now. It was never any enchantment on me — just you. You struck a bargain with the architect, and he let you have just enough power to keep me from leaving the tower. Now he's dead, and your bargain is done."

You are such a stupid, stupid man.

"Whatever you say. If we wait here, Uzhdon will find us, and he will cut me to bits, and you will be stuck here in this tower of blood, in this place where they entomb gods alive. Your choice."

He felt her fury, a hundred thunderstorms, a shedding snake. The very air before his eyes seemed to vibrate with it. Then it was suddenly gone, her anger as fickle as everything else about her. For an instant a vision of her swallowed his senses — naked, supple, hard-muscled, soft-fleshed, straddling down on him, tangled hair falling across her face, green eyes flashing, mouth curving in terrible glee, breasts pressing against his own chest with shivering heat, and the scent of her flesh as it sank against and into his own.

She laughed, and the image vanished. Later, then. Later. And the gates of his heart shut again. His fear was gone, and he went down the rope like a monkey. It was midday, but he didn't care.

He came up thirty feet short of the street, but a cart full of melons passed under him, so he kicked out from the wall and let go, landing amongst the fruit with a wet sound. Ignoring the vendor's inarticulate curses, he climbed out of the sticky mess and down onto the street.

Something hit the ground next to him. It was a chunk of brick.

He looked up. The tower was swaying weirdly, like a tall cane in a high wind.

He figured it was time to leave. He ran up the mildewed streets of Rumq Qaj and didn't look back, even when he heard a sound like an avalanche.

Outside of the city gates, he stopped running. Everyone was going the other way to see what was happening, making it fairly simple for him to acquire a horse, one with well-provisioned saddlebags already strapped on.

Would Uzhdon stay to destroy the other buildings, or had Fool Wolf given the hero a better, more important cause? Whichever, he imagined he had a pretty good head start. It was bound to take a few hours, at least, to dig out from under a fallen god.

The Python King's Treasure

FOOL WOLF ONLY HAD a few days left to live when he saw the most beautiful woman he had ever laid eyes upon.

Her hair was spun black glass, spilling down the sides of a face incised from amber, flowing over shoulders and down breasts of the same red-gold hue.

He was too far away to see what color her eyes were, but he could feel her gaze on him. She stood on the edge of a cliff, half a bow-shot above him, looking down at the jade sea and the cinnamon sun it was swallowing in the west.

And at him, on the desolate strand, fifteen days along the way to starvation.

He stood rooted, stunned, watching her naked lithe half-shadow in the melting sunlight.

She is pretty, the goddess imprisoned in him sighed, wistfully. She looks good enough to eat.

Fool Wolf's stomach growled in agreement.

✣ ✣ ✣

A month earlier, in the Land of Nine Princes, in the many-tiered city of Fanva, Fool Wolf had been considerably better-fed. He had arrived in Fanva with a single carnelian and two copper coins, fleeing from the blood-guttered city of Rumq Qaj. In the incense-choked gambling temples of Fanva, he had increased that jewel and those two coins into what was for him a small fortune. He took a room in a good inn, draped himself in silk and feasted on roast pork, pheasant, peacock, and eel. He ate sweet fruits from the islands — Lom, whitemelon, fernpears, bananas. He drank wines he could not name but which pleased him a great deal and a bedded a series of women of the same sort.

His fortunes changed, of course. He was caught cheating by one of the gambling-house priests. As gambling was a religious matter in Fanva, and cheating sacrilege, he was sentenced to death.

While bets were being placed on which form of death would be chosen and how long he would survive, Fool Wolf escaped his would-be-executioners and fled into the Gibbering Quarter, where foreign diplomats and madmen lived. He eluded his pursuit through the open window of a third story apartment, waiting breathlessly for distance to hush their cries and footsteps, alert for any movement by the occupants of his refuge.

None came, and after five hundred heartbeats, he began to explore. It was a large place, well furnished with exotic rugs, censers of gold and cream-colored ivory, screens of lacquered wood and stippled velum. It smelled strange, like burnt sugar candy and wet dog.

And books, everywhere. Crammed into shelves, littered in the rugs and polished wooden floors, piled on low sitting-desks.

Behind one of those desks sat a dead man. He hadn't been dead long — drool was still leaking from his mouth. His flesh was still warm.

Fool Wolf could see no obvious reason why the man died, unless it was the small, empty cordial glass on the table before of him. Suicide by poison, or just a last drink before dying from some natural cause? Probably the first — aside from being dead, the corpse did not look unhealthy. In fact, he looked something like an older Fool Wolf — tall and lean, narrow of face with sharp, high cheekbones, long black hair plaited into a queue.

That meant the dead man's clothes would probably fit Fool Wolf. He began rummaging about the apartment and shortly found a closet full of green robes. He took one and found it fit rather well, so he cast about for further items of disguise. A turban, of course, and something to make a false beard with, perhaps.

He congratulated himself on his luck. It looked as if no one else lived here — there were no woman's clothes, no servants quarters. The dead man seemed to have lived alone. He could keep his head down here until the pursuit cooled.

He had just settled onto a comfortable cushion with a plate of olives when the door splintered inward. Fool Wolf froze, an olive halfway to his mouth.

Standing in the doorframe was a rather large man in a black fighting sarong and loose, blood-red shirt. His arms, visible from the elbow, were covered in elaborate tattoos. On his forehead was a single tattoo, the glyph of a tiger chasing its own tail. A long, curved sword gleamed in his sash.

The black-clad man walked into the room, followed by two hulking eunuchs that made him look like a dwarf, and ten guardsmen behind them. All had the tiger tattoo.

"Lohar Pang?" The man in black said. It sounded something like a question.

Fool Wolf pursed his lips. The corpse was in the next room. If they went in there . . .

"Of course," he replied. "Lohar Pang, at your service."

"Wonderful. You will come with us."

"I'm busy at the moment," Fool Wolf replied, bowing.

"Ah. My apologies," the man in black said. "I misstated myself. You will come with us, or you will die."

"Oh," Fool Wolf said, "this is a day for misstatement, for I'm not busy at all. Shall we go?"

✠ ✠ ✠

Fool Wolf had heard of Prince Fa — few in Fanva had not. He wasn't one of the nine princes, but he was a merchant of considerable power and reportedly dark tastes. He looked about sixty, with a trim beard and sooty eyes. He wore a robe so deeply red it was almost black, bordered with twining serpents and eels picked out in garnet. His throne was of heavy dun wood and would have been rather plain if not for the human skulls along the armrests and high back. Into each skull twenty or so nails had been driven. Fool Wolf suspected that this had been done when the heads were still breathing and blinking and screaming. Prince Fa frowned down at Fool Wolf, then examined his long, gold-leafed nails. "This should be a simple task, for one of your repute," the prince said, flashing teeth like bits of polished abalone. "You have familiarized yourself with the — problem — and with the gods in question? You examined the objects I sent you?"

"Absolutely," Fool Wolf said, wondering what in the name of the Horse Mother prince Fa was talking about.

"And you still say you can do it?"

"Of course. I have no doubts."

"Good. Then you will live. You will depart immediately." He leaned forward, and his shadowed eyes caught the flicker of a candle flame, a red fish in deep water. "If I have to take a hand in this myself, I will be most displeased," Fa murmured. "I detest the sea. You understand the consequences if I am forced to do something I hate?"

"Of course, prince Fa," Fool Wolf said, wondering what the consequences were, imagining they were unpleasant.

"Good. One of my yachts is prepared to leave."

It occurred to Fool Wolf that a trip by boat would at least get him far from the city. After that — well, there would surely be opportunities.

✛ ✛ ✛

A week later, he was still watching for the first of those hypothetical opportunities. More specifically, he was gazing at the horizon, wondering how big the ocean could be.

Too big to swim, he kept coming back to. So even though he was unwatched by the crew — somewhat avoided, even — there was no place to escape to.

Kreth — the black-saronged warrior from the apartment — joined him at the rail.

"Not much farther," Kreth said, spitting onto the sky-dressed sea, watching the little foam island thus created break up in the ship's wake. "Can you really do it?"

"I've never failed before," Fool Wolf assured him.

"Obviously. But you've never been to Ranga Lehau before, either," Kreth grunted. "Still, the prince seems pretty sure of you. He read one of your treatises or somesuch. How will you do it?"

"How do you imagine I will do it?" Fool Wolf asked.

"You don't have to be mysterious," Kreth replied, a bit sulkily. "If you can't tell me, just say so."

"I can't tell you, but you can guess, and I can nod yes or no."

"Never mind then. I'm not good at such games, and I shall see, shortly, yes?" He reached over and gave Fool Wolf a slap on the back that clacked his teeth together. "But you can do it?"

"Of course." Fool Wolf glanced over at Kreth. "What's your part in all of this? Aside from making sure I do my part?"

"I'm the hunter," Kreth replied. "I will find the Tattooed Python King's treasure, never fear. He cannot hide it from me."

"I don't doubt that for a moment," Fool Wolf replied.

That's all Fool Wolf got from Kreth, and the hunter was too smart to push any further. Fool Wolf didn't want to ask a question that raised even minor suspicion — he didn't know what Lohar Pang was supposed to know. As long as he was on this boat, with nothing but sea around, he might as well be in prince Fa's palace.

⁜ ⁜ ⁜

Thus it was, two days later, when Kreth came to Fool Wolf's cabin and said, "It is time," he still didn't have a fart's whisper of what it was time for.

Up on deck, Kreth pointed to the first land Fool Wolf had seen since the coastline of Fanva faded in the west. It was an island, looking something like a giant black horse tooth sticking up out of the water, with its sheer black cliffs and flat top.

"That is Ranga Lehau," Kreth commented. "According to our charts, we cross the tapu when we pass those rocks."

Fool Wolf saw the rocks he meant, two pillars of stone jutting up from the water, perhaps three ship's lengths apart. They looked manmade. At the rate the boat was moving, they would reach them soon.

As Fool Wolf studied the rocks and the island, Kreth shuffled impatiently. "Shouldn't you get started?" He asked. He sounded nervous.

"Don't tell me my business," Fool Wolf snapped. Then, a bit more mysteriously, "besides, I have started."

"Oh. I thought there would be more — chanting, or something."

"In a moment," Fool Wolf said. "If you will kindly darken your mouth."

The rocks were closer. "Chugaachik!" Fool Wolf chanted. "Do you have any idea what these fools want of me?" He sang in his own tongue, Mang, not a language anyone else on the ship was likely to know.

I don't know, the goddess answered, in that silent place between his breaths. Why not let me kill them all? That would solve the problem.

"Because I don't think we can kill them all, even with your power," he sang.

That was a half-truth. He hated Chugaachik, who had killed most everyone he had ever loved and made him a rootless wanderer, far from his native land. She just might be able to kill everyone on the ship, but letting her have her way, even to save his life, was not something he was willing to do unless he knew he had no choice.

Besides, it was his body she used, his body that paid for her excesses.

They were almost to the pillars.

But, Chugaachik offered reluctantly, there is a large and powerful god crouching there, beneath the water.

The sea raised up in a mound, and the nose of the boat tilted with it. Fool Wolf ran and jumped as far as he could toward the island. When he hit the water, he began stroking furiously, ignoring the brief screams and rending of wood behind him.

✠ ✠ ✠

Fifteen days later none of the bodies or supplies from the ship had washed ashore, anywhere. He knew — he had made a compete circuit of the island. In the four days it had taken, Fool Wolf had seen no sign of human life and no way to the plateau above him.

And now this impossible woman, gazing down at him from that unattainable place.

"Hello!" He shouted. "Hello up there! Can you help me?"

She cocked her head to the side but otherwise merely continued to stare.

"Pakena lafa? Em'tagi?" He croaked, trying Jara and Fanvese. She didn't respond any more than she had to Mang.

"Please," he tried again, "I was shipwrecked and haven't eaten in half a moon."

The woman regarded him for a bit longer, as if he was some strange shorebird with an odd call. Then she turned and walked out of sight, into the forest at the top of the cliff.

✠ ✠ ✠

For a little while, Fool Wolf nurtured the hope that the woman was coming down for him, following some secret path or tunnel in the rock he hadn't found. She would bring all sorts of things from the paradise above. Whitemelon, roast pig, chicken, deer. Bread. Beer. Wine. The comfort of her flesh, the sweet touch of her lips . . .

But the sea went from jade to obsidian, and the sky opened its six thousand eyes, and still she did not come. Fool Wolf felt as if he was made of driftwood. Perhaps when he became light enough, the wind would pick him up and he could fly to the top.

✠ ✠ ✠

By the time morning greened the eastern sky, he had given up. Whoever the woman was, she hadn't been as impressed with the sight of Fool Wolf as he had been with her. Of course he was half starved, his normally coppery skin burned almost teak and his long black hair in brine-petrified knots. He could hardly blame her if she didn't like what she saw.

Well, no, that wasn't true. He was dying. He did blame her. Her, and the gambling priests, and prince Fa, and Kreth, and every sailor and soldier on the lost boat.

And he blamed the island, of course. From the sea it had looked green and inviting. But all of the green was at the top of those walls of glassy rock. That left him with a narrow strip of sterile white beach, two to twenty paces wide, a few rocky spurs into the sea supporting nothing more edible than barnacles, seagulls he hadn't devised any way to catch, fish that must be out there but which he couldn't find or see in the foaming surf. And he wasn't going too far into that surf, now with whatever-it-was lurking out there.

But if she was up there, that indifferent beauty, there must be a way up — a way he had missed in his four-day circuit of the island.

So, cursing, he went to his one source of sustenance — a small freshwater spring seeping from the base of the cliff. He drank as much as his belly would hold and then started walking. If he remembered correctly, the next spring was more than a day away.

☩ ☩ ☩

A couple of things occurred to him while walking.

The first was that the woman — and whatever other people lived atop the island — might come and go by rope, or ladder, or not at all. Of course, the first time someone went up, there must have been a natural way, but that might have been a thousand years ago.

A more serious worry was that he might not have seen a woman at all. It might have been a ghost, or a goddess, a shapeshifter — or his hungry imagination.

He spent a lot of time studying the edge of the cliff, but he didn't see her again.

The next day he reached the river. He remembered the spot well, because it had been so frustrating. The cliffs here were lower than anywhere else on the island. If he could jump twice again his own height, he would be able to catch the tree roots straggling over the rim. At the lowest point, a waterfall tumbled mockingly into a pool and then flowed out to the waiting ocean. He had looked here for hours, searching for handholds, and finding none. No fish in the water, either.

The waterfall had worn a deep grove for itself — a narrow canyon, really. Standing at the base of it, he could curl his fingers onto the top of the ledge the water came over. But with the water pushing down on him, and the stone even smoother than elsewhere, he could never get enough purchase to pull himself up more than a finger's breadth.

He wasn't going to waste his time on it again.

That was when he noticed the falls looked strange. The water was bumping up, flowing over something. He trudged closer.

A dead tree was wedged in the mouth of the waterfall.

✟ ✟ ✟

He caught the branch on his third jump, but his muscles had nothing in them, and he just hung there, water battering him.

Let me help you, the Chugaachik said.

'No. If I do, then you'll kill her. And anyone else up there."

Probably. But why should you care? She left you to die.

Chugaachik had a point. But instead of calling on her help, he pulled again, knowing it was his last chance. If he failed, he would have to let Chugaachik have him.

I won't eat her right away, the goddess promised. I'll let you have her body first. I know you want it.

His arms trembled, and he almost gave up. Then he remembered the last time the goddess had been loose in his body — and what they had done together — and found some extra strength, enough for one great heave that allowed him to hook his arm over the wedged log. Another, lesser jerk, and he had a leg over, too.

He lay that way for a moment, draped over the log, suddenly, absurdly happy. He managed to cough out a series of chuckles, while garnering his energy to move again.

The river broadened upstream, and the canyon walls here were still too steep to climb. But the banks of the river were wide enough to walk on, and gently sloping, and ahead he could see the waving fronds of fernpear trees.

He crawled onto the bank and began to walk.

Fifty paces from the dark, inviting jungle, he came across four wooden statues, each about the size of himself, carved from tree-trunks. They were very old, standing at odd angles, half rotted, made to resemble little squatting men with big heads.

Beyond them was a town. Or rather, the remains of a town. The roofs of the enormous buildings had caved in and creeping vines covered their skeletons.

At another time, that might interest him. Not now. All he cared about was food.

He took three more steps, and one of the statues spoke to him. It didn't move its rotted wooden lips, but the words appear just inside his ear, like a bee buzzing there.

You are not Talehau, the voice whirred.

"Sure I am," Fool Wolf asserted.

No. We know the lineages, and you are not of them.

"All I want is some food from the forest."

You might be a pirate. You might be a thief. You have a powerful spirit in you. We will not let you enter Lehau.

"The village? Look behind you! They are all dead! You guard nothing!"

No, the statue replied. One remains. As long as one remains, we guard.

Fool Wolf gritted his teeth. The woman! That damned woman again!

"I ignore you now," he told the statues, and strode briskly past them.

✠ ✠ ✠

He came to in the river, his limbs twitching like dying eels, sparks dancing before his eyes.

With a horrible start, he realized that he was fetched up against the log, about to float over it and back down the waterfall.

He flopped back onto the bank.

"Okay," he panted to Chugaachik. "Okay. Help me. Do whatever you want."

For the first time since he was a boy, he got no answer, not even a purr or a growl.

His heart did a strange twist in his breast. Was he finally rid of her? For years he had been fleeing the consequences of Chugaachik's actions and searching for a shaman powerful enough to release the goddess from his body. How ironic it would be to be free now, just before starving to death.

He trudged back up the slope to confront the statues again.

You are not Talehau, they reminded him.

"No. But I mean no harm. I just need food. Can't I just walk inland for a little while, if I promise to come right back out?"

No.

Fool Wolf felt dizzy. There must be some way to argue with these intractable gods, but he needed rest before he thought of it. Now that he was up here, he certainly wasn't going back down.

✠ ✠ ✠

He awoke, then scrambled wildly away from the snake nudging him in the side.

Only it wasn't a snake, he saw, as the foolish colors of sleep leaked from his eyes. It was a long piece of bamboo, and holding the other end of it was the woman.

The sight of her knocked the breath right out of him. She was crouched down, just beyond the guardian gods. She had wrapped some sort of kilt around her waist, but it didn't conceal much of her. And he could see her eyes now. They were the color the smoke would be if you could burn jade.

"Hello," he said softly. "It's nice to see you again."

She didn't answer, but she let the stick drop. Maybe she had been wondering if he was dead.

"I need a favor," Fool Wolf said, carefully. "Something to eat. Could you do that for me?" He pantomimed chewing, then thumped his belly. It thudded like a shaman's drum.

She watched him as he repeated himself in several languages, then got up and swayed off into the forest. He watched her long, shapely legs and thought of them crisped over a fire and served with rice.

Fool Wolf folded back down by the statues.

"Will you answer some questions?" He asked the guardians wearily.

Yes.

"Of all the people you once guarded, only one is still alive?"

True. Save for one, the Talehau are no more.

"What happened to them?"

My brothers and I were tree spirits. Long ago, when the Talehau first arrived here, we struck a bargain with them. They would refrain from cutting trees — beyond a certain allotted number — and we would guard them from enemies. We could not protect them from themselves, however. The tattooed Python King, whose island this is, fell in love with a woman of the village and took her to live with him. Her brother Mahan, a proud and jealous man, heard of this. He sought his sister for months. When he found her, she told him she loved the Python King. The brother, who desired his sister, swore that if he could not have her, no one should. So Mahan killed her, to spite the King. In his rage, the Python King slew everyone on the island — all but one, for he wanted one to carry the memory of what had happened. Then he swore enmity to Humans and put the tapu around the island.

Fool Wolf tried to absorb all of that. There were a lot of questions there, but what was most important right now was getting past the guardians.

"Ah — when the Talehau had visitors from other islands — not pirates, just visitors — did you let them pass?"

Of course. If they were greeted by the Talehau or the gods of this island — if we could be sure they were guests, you see, and not interlopers.

"I see. Well — I'm harmless enough. I'm sure you can see that. And you are gods. Can't you invite me in?"

It is against our bargain to do so, of course.

"Of course."

But he could get her to invite him in. If she could talk, which he had seen no evidence of.

"How long ago was Lehau abandoned?"

"Twenty years ago."

Fool Wolf nodded. The woman didn't look a sliver-moon over twenty-five. If she had been alone since the age of five and hadn't spoken to another human being since then, maybe she couldn't talk at all.

But maybe she could, or he could teach her.

So he took a bath. It wasn't easy — he was weak, and the current, though not strong by any normal standards, was too rapid for him. He dipped water out with his hands, then lay on the bank, ducking his head under, working the salty tangles in his hair out with his fingers.

He threw away the remains of his robe. Maybe, if she could see his wasting body, she would feel sorry for him. Or, if she had never seen a man before, perhaps she would be curious. If she came back.

And she did come back, near sundown, with a heavy netted bag. His heart thudded with glee as brightly colored fruit, steaming banana-leaf bundles, and a dead chicken spilled onto the ground. The woman set about gathering wood for a fire, as Fool Wolf licked his lips.

"I can help you with that, if you just invite me over," He called. "Weak as I am, I would be glad to do the work of building a fire."

She gave no indication that she heard him.

"Very well — I understand. You have no reason to trust me. But you must like me — see, you brought me food. It's very nice of you to cook, but I wonder if I could have some of the fruit now?"

He might have been talking to the sea.

Soon he was panting like a dog at the scent of the bird roasting on a spit. He had never smelled anything better. In front of him, she ate every bit of the food. When she was done, she considered the bird carcass, picked off what remained of the meat, and tossed the bones at Fool Wolf. Then she threw the rinds of the fruit at him to.

"You bitch!" Fool Wolf shrieked, pouncing on the remains.

He ate the rinds, though they were bitter. He ate the bones, too, smashing them and sucking out what remained of the marrow.

An hour later, he threw it up, and for the first time she made a sound.

She laughed, then walked away again.

✠ ✠ ✠

She repeated her performance the next day, and the next. By the fourth day he didn't even bother to stir — it was a waste of energy.

"I wonder why you do this too me," Fool Wolf said. "I wonder how you can hate me so, when I have done you no harm." He watched her tear a drumstick from a chicken and take a large bite. He could hear the skin crackle, see the grease dribble down her beautiful chin.

"But you can't even understand me, can you? You're just like some poor dumb beast."

"No," she said, in Jara, or a language very like it. "I can talk."

"Then why —"

"I have little to say to you. You came here to kill me, yes? My father always said someone would."

"Not me. I'm just a castaway."

"Yes, from the boat the Python King destroyed. The one that violated the tapu."

"I know nothing of this. I was just a passenger, and an unwilling one at that."

"I don't believe you."

"What's your name?" he asked.

"Why do you want to know?"

"Because you are the loveliest woman I have ever seen. Because if you are going to kill me, you at least owe me the name of my murderer, so I can tell it to my ancestors."

"Names are too important for me to give you mine. And you murdered yourself by coming here. It isn't my fault." She smiled, faintly. "You came for the Tattooed Python King's treasure, didn't you?"

"I heard my captors mention that, yes."

"I am the Python King's treasure. So you came to kill or kidnap me. You see? I do have something against you. You aren't the first, you know." She tossed another cleaned carcass over the tapu line. It was difficult, but he ignored it.

"You are undeniably a treasure," Fool Wolf said, "but I did not come here for you. Though allow me to say — if you were mine, and not this Python King's, I would treasure you indeed. I have been to fabulous Nhol and ancient Lhe, to Rumq Qaj, Palipurn, and Fanva. I have seen the great mountain in Balati and the high plains of Falling Sky. I have walked most of this world, yet I have never seen any jewel or star as beautiful as your eyes. I have known many woman, but next to you even the loveliest might as well have been a man. And now that I have heard you speak, no harp or flute —"

She was smiling, a fascinated little smile. "How long can you keep that up?" She asked.

"I could praise your beauty to the end of my days," he answered. "Unfortunately, that won't be in the very distant future."

"Hmm." She considered that for a moment, then rolled a whitemelon toward him. It stopped just inside the tapu line — on his side. He stared at it, shaking, fearing a trick.

"Go on," she said. "You've pleased me."

He took the melon and split it open. The smell of the sweet white meat nearly overpowered him.

He gobbled it down and wiped his mouth. "May I have another?" He asked.

"Talk to me a little more, and you may."

"Your thighs are like —"

"No. Not about me. I know what I look like. Tell me more about those places. Those cities and such."

"Oh. Well — there's Nhol, Nhol of the white pyramids, which gleam in the sun as if they were made of eggshells —"

☩ ☩ ☩

A week later, he was starting to feel less hungry. His flesh was beginning to gain substance again, though she was still miserly with what she gave him.

"Why don't you invite me over there?" He asked. "You must know by now I wouldn't hurt you."

"I know from your stories you are a thief and a liar," she said.

"I never said any such thing."

"No. You dance around it, but it's always there. You are a faithless and fickle man, Fool Wolf. How can I trust you?"

"Because I've changed. My love for you has changed me."

She laughed. "You love me no more than you have ever loved any woman, I'll guess. You do like the look of me, I think, but then that isn't love, is it?"

"What would you know about it? Have you ever even known a man?"

"Others have been where you are now. All were faithless."

A little chill bristled across his scalp. "I am not them."

"I've heard stories, too."

"From who?"

She shrugged. "I hear stories. That's all."

She tossed him a packet of steamed breadfruit, and was silent while he devoured it.

"Tell me," she said. "If I allowed it — what would you do, if I let you come over here? If I let you love me?"

He looked up at that, at her supple, gleaming limbs, at the swell of her breasts. "That's cruel," Fool Wolf said. "That's worse than making me watch you eat when I'm starving."

"No it isn't. Or would you like to compare? I can always stop feeding you."

"No!" he said quickly. "No! I — ah — don't you want to hear more about my travels?"

"No. I want to hear the other, now."

He put away the remains of the breadfruit and crept as near the tapu boundary as he could. He fixed his eyes on her.

"Well," he murmured, reaching his hand up, as if to touch her, " — I would first caress your arms with the tips of my fingers, until little bumps rose up on them. And then . . ."

☦ ☦ ☦

That night he lay awake, unable to sleep. He was getting used to the strange night noises of the island, but his mind was working and would not let him rest.

He'd almost had her, today. He could see it in her eyes. Soon she would invite him across. Then he could start thinking about a building a boat. Maybe there were old maps in the ruined village.

He shook that off — it was too many steps down the road. For now, the goal was much simpler — to not have to depend on her for his life.

He shifted his eyes at a slight sound, saw a shadow gliding.

She was about ten paces from him, a ghost in the moonlight. He kept very still.

"Listen to me," she said. "I still haven't invited you over the tapu line. If you hurt me, or kill me, you will starve here. Do you understand that? There is no one else to care for you."

"I would not hurt you," Fool Wolf replied.

"Good. Then I want — I want some of those things you talked about."

"Really? And then you will invite me over?"

"I promise nothing. But maybe."

"Come here, then," Fool Wolf said, "and you will see that I make good on my promises." He reached for her leg, and stroked along the inner calf. She made an odd sound, and after a moment, her knees buckled, and she knelt next to him.

He pressed his face into the hollow of her neck, and his face and belly prickled at the scent of her skin.

"My name is Inah," she murmured.

After that, she made more odd sounds. Many more.

✠ ✠ ✠

One more awakening, one more rude surprise. This one was a sharp kick in the ribs and a curse. Fool Wolf opened his eyes in time to see Inah flee back over the tapu line.

"Liar!" She shrieked.

"What?" Fool Wolf yelped, staggering to his feet and clutching his aching flank. "What did I do?"

She lifted her chin and pointed with it. "Your friends are here," she said.

He turned. Beyond the waterfall, in the slice of ocean he could see, was a large boat, very much like the boat he had come on.

Prince Fa, or more of his men. Inside the tapu.

"No!" He shouted. "They are my enemies, too. Invite me over! Don't leave me out here!"

For an instant she seemed to consider it, then tossed her black mane contemptuously. "You almost tricked me," she said. Then she vanished into the jungle.

✠ ✠ ✠

"I've been waiting for you," Fool Wolf said.

Prince Fa did not look happy. None of the two-score soldiers with him looked happy, either.

"Have you." The Prince said, frostily. "What happened to my other ship? And Kreth, and the others?"

"The tapu got them."

"But it didn't get you, the sorcerer who was supposed to deal with it. How coincidental. Have you secured the treasure yet?"

Fool Wolf remembered the night, the fierce tangling of limbs. "In a manner of speaking."

"Where is she, then?"

"I don't know."

The Prince smiled, very narrowly. "Things aren't going well for you, whoever you are. Lohar's body was found, you know, which reveals you as a fraud. Your lies have lost me a good ship and some very good men. You may remember, too, what I said about having to take a hand in matters myself. It cost me more than I care to say to quiet the Python King and his tapu. Even so, he won't stay quiet for long. So where is she?"

"If I knew, I would tell you. She ran into the jungle when you came."

Fa cocked his head. "But she was here? You talked to her?" His face transfigured, slightly. "Oh, I see. More than that. Well. You shall live a little longer then." He signed to his men. "Bind his hands but leave his feet free."

A heavyset thug lashed Fool Wolf's hands together with leather straps. Meanwhile, Prince Fa approached the sentinel statues. Fool Wolf braced himself. When the Prince collapsed, he would take advantage of the confusion and flee back to the beach. If he could swim out to the ship, defeat whoever was on board . . .

He needed Chugaachik now, but he was beginning to think she was really gone.

The prince wandered beyond the sentinels. He turned and looked at his soldiers and Fool Wolf. "It's safe," he said. "All of you come with me."

✛ ✛ ✛

They didn't go far. In the old square of the ruined village, Fa's men cleared the jungle growth and then, at the edge of the clearing, they hung Fool Wolf between two trees. They built a fire and amused themselves by searing his flesh with brands.

Fool Wolf was Mang by birth — his people were fierce horsemen who raised their children to expect and endure torture.

Fool Wolf had never been a very good Mang, and he was weak already. After a time, he screamed, and screamed again. When they thought he had screamed enough, they cut him down, bound him to one of the trees, and made camp some distance away.

Fool Wolf watched the moon rise.

"Chugaachik?" He whispered. "Are you really gone?" He got no answer. He watched the moon set.

And with the largest eyes of heaven closed, Inah came.

"What have they done to you?" She whispered.

"Go away," he said. "This is what they want. They want you to try to help me."

"I'm sorry I didn't believe you," she said. Her fingers traced upon his face, and he could just make out her eyes.

"Inah, run."

"They cannot stop me. You don't know everything about me. I . . . " her voice stumbled and she made a little choking noise. "What?" She gasped. She sounded confused. Then she slid against Fool Wolf, across his burned flesh, and fell in a heap at his feet.

"Well!" Prince Fa's voice came out of the darkness. "Congratulations! You proved useful after all."

"I'm going to kill you, Fa," Fool Wolf said.

"Of course you are."

"What did you do to her?"

"An extract of the poison of the Hutoew tree. She will live."

"Why? What do you want from her?"

Fa's face appeared in a little glow of witchlight from something in his hand. Fool Wolf looked down and saw Inah: she had two small darts in her neck. Her eyes were open, glassy.

"At first I just wanted her. Now, I want something more. I suppose I should thank you for forcing me to come here, to conquer my fears. Yes, my fears! I had not realized how powerful I have become. So I will allow you live a while, and let you dream of killing me. Such dreams are sweet, are they not? It is my reward to you, to see me fulfill mine." He turned to his men, who had been gathering behind him.

"Bind her, and complete the circle around them."

"Aren't we going, now that we have her?" One of the men asked.

"No," Fa said. "We await one more."

✠ ✠ ✠

Fool Wolf sought for Chugaachik one last time, knowing that if he did not find her he would die, and so would Inah. Of course, if he did find Chugaachik, Inah might die anyway. Chugaachik did not treat Fool Wolf's lovers well, generally.

Fool Wolf's father had wanted him to be a gaan, a shaman. That was how Fool Wolf had ended up with a goddess living in him. And though he had long ago abandoned his father's path for him, he still had enough training to set his spirit drifting into the world-beneath-the-surface-of-the-world, the world of spirit.

He went about aimlessly, at first, in the dark counterpart of the island. He walked hard beaten paths where the gaunt dead roamed in circles.

It might have been days or ten heartbeats of wandering before he found the guardians, but find them he finally did. Here they were four old men, balding and bearded, with flesh like knotted wood. They watched him approach with little half-smiles.

"Hello again," one said.

"Hello, grandfathers. I'm looking for something."

"That being?"

"The goddess that accompanied me to the island."

"Ah. She is with the Python King. She fled your body when we touched you. The King found her before she could return."

"And where is he? The Python King?"

They sent him through a forest of wailing trees and dark, scurrying things, through a marsh where slender cranes that looked liked wrought iron fished for souls, and at last to a high peak with a bowl-shaped valley at the top. All along the rim were the remains of shrines, low platforms with small standing stones. Clustered around the shrines, like ants around fruit, were Human ghosts, sitting with their heads between their knees, some weeping. One looked up at Fool Wolf with eyes like the empty space in a chrysalis, once the moth is gone.

"Help me," the ghost said.

Fool Wolf uttered a single, bitter laugh and continued on. But he thought he heard something, now. A faint voice, speaking his name. He tried to follow the sound, but it never seemed to get any louder or softer, and he could never be certain that it really was his name.

Until the melodic baritone suddenly spoke it right in his ear.

"Fool Wolf, I suppose?"

He turned. The speaker was a handsome man of middle years, densely muscled. He wore a crimson sarong, but the rest of his dark body was clothed only in tattoos, the mottled spots of a python.

"And you are the Python King?"

"That is one of my names. I expected to see you sooner."

"Prince Fa said he had put you to sleep."

The Python King blinked as if waking from a dream. "Fa? Fa? He is not that powerful. But Fa is not his name, and he has hidden his name from me. Hiding that, he has hidden himself. I cannot see him, or even long hold the thought of him before me. Now he is calling me, and I am compelled to go into his trap. I will forget as I go. I fear he will kill me then, and you, and take Inah away."

"There is nothing you can do? They say you made this island. You must have more power than that."

The Python King shrugged and clasped his hands behind his back. "An island is a small thing, really. And in those days creating was easier. I have lived here too long, forgotten too much. This man — you see, I cannot even remember what you called him, now — he has studied arts unknown in my day. I do not ken them."

"Fa. His name is Fa. He came here to steal your treasure and to kill you."

"And so he shall. And his name is not Fa."

Fool Wolf sighed. "You have something of mine."

"Oh, yes," the Python king said. "Her. Do you really want her back?"

"No. But I think I have no other choice."

"I suppose you don't. Though I suspect that she won't be able to help, much." Behind him and a jackal stalked out of the forest. A gray jackal mottled black, the size of a horse, with red carbuncle eyes.

"Hello, sweet thing," Chugaachik said. "You missed me."

Fool Wolf ignored her. "Can you put her back in me? Back in my Mansion of Bone?"

The Python King looked at him for a moment, then reached for Chugaachik. He lifted her by the scruff of the neck and shook her once, hard, so that she became a long pelt. He rolled her up and squeezed her into a small, black jewel.

"Swallow it," the god told him. "Or not. I have to go now. Someone is calling me."

"Prince Fa?"

"I only know I must go."

The god lifted and flowed, a sinuous smoke, a great snake in the sky. Fool Wolf caught his tail and went with him.

Soon he saw the clearing, and his body, and Inah.

He lifted the jewel to his mouth and paused. Wouldn't it be better to die than to have Chugaachik in him again?

No.

He swallowed the jewel and smelled a sharp tang like wet metal or a bloody nose. He felt scratching, like a spider beneath his tongue. And, of course, her laughter, shrill, and a surge of desire that was only a little like lust for a woman.

He woke to his flesh.

But it wasn't his flesh for long.

✛ ✛ ✛

He was still bound, but a grin stretched itself from ear to ear. His teeth felt like obsidian knives. His fingers were talons. And the rope that bound him — rotten string.

Prince Fa stood before him, seemingly oblivious to the changes working in Fool Wolf.

"Well," the Prince said, beaming, waving a curved, bloody sword. "You awake just in time. See who I have before me." He gestured. A huge Python, the length of thirty men, lay near where Inah hung. Its head was hacked halfway off, but it was still alive, writhing, golden blood bubbling from its nostrils.

"He doesn't even know I'm here," Fa said, his voice full of delight.

Chugaachik chuckled, and it came out of Fool Wolf's mouth. Let me have him, she demanded.

Not yet, he told her. He may be too much even for you. Just wait a bit, and I promise you —

You will not cheat me again, the goddess said.

I surely will. But not this time. This time, I need you.

Fa had turned his attention back to the great snake, and lifted his sword to strike again.

"I bet he would recognize you if I told him your name," Fool Wolf said.

Fa stopped, glanced at him, and for an instant, Fool Wolf saw fear there. Fa pointed the sword at him. "Shut up," he said.

Something clamped upon Fool Wolf's vocal cords. Fa stepped forward and raised the sword for a blow that would decapitate Fool Wolf. "Just in case you do know," Fa said.

Now, he told Chugaachik.

Now? Chugaachik screamed. You idiot! Black lightning uncoiled. And as he lost his voice, and his limbs, and his mind to the goddess and her desires, he shouted to the Python King.

"Mahan!" He told the god. "His name is Mahan!"

Then Fa's blade struck him. Chugaachik had managed, in that less than a heartbeat, to snap the bonds and bring his arms up. The blade sank through flesh and shattered the bone of his right forearm, allowing the blade to bite into the side of his neck. Something splashed wetly on his shoulder.

Fool Wolf snarled.

Fa's eyes widened, and he swung again, shouting something at the same moment. Fool Wolf lunged at him, but met with a peculiar slipperiness. His claws would not catch — it was as if the Prince were made of glass.

And the sword hit him again, this time crunching its way through several ribs. Fool Wolf screamed, a scream of pure fury, and looked up into the deathblow dropping toward his face.

At that moment a great coil engulfed Fa. His surprised look was suddenly hidden by another coil whipping around to the top of that one, and then the head of a great serpent, darted down, teeth gleaming.

Fa had men. Some were running, while others were coming forward to help their master. All moved as if walking through syrup.

Blood pumping from his arms, neck and side, Fool Wolf launched himself at them. Their terror was sweet, but not as sweet as their blood. He eviscerated every one.

Then he turned on Inah, full of joy and anticipation.

He slipped in blood, and to his disgust found that he did not have the strength to get up. The small part of him that was really Fool Wolf rejoiced.

✠ ✠ ✠

You still owe me! Chugaachik howled, somewhere. You did trick me! You almost let him kill us!

You had your way with his men. Be satisfied with that. "Be satisfied that we're still alive," he finished, aloud.

"A gift from my father," another voice said. Inah, who was wiping his forehead with a damp cloth. He lay on a barkcloth mat, in a dimly lit hut.

"The Python King. Your father."

"Yes, of course. He mended the worst of your wounds, made water into blood for you." She bent over and kissed him. "I'm sorry for the way I treated you. If I had known you would save my life — and my father's life — I would have been much nicer from the beginning. But I thought you were him."

"Fa? Mahan? The man who killed your mother?"

"Did he?" she wrinkled her brow. "Father only told me that he let one villager live, and that it was a man. He didn't say who it was. How did you know?"

"I guessed. All along I thought you were the last villager, the one the Python King let live. But you aren't. You aren't even human."

"I'm half human. I seemed human enough the other night, didn't I? You didn't know, then."

"No. But you are of your father's lineage, not of the village. It was only when Fa — Mahan — passed the guardians without even a struggle that I understood. Who better to remember the crime than the criminal?" He shook his head. "A mistake. Gods are too fond of poetics and curses. This irony turned itself on your father. It almost killed him." A sudden thought occurred. "Fa's boat — what happened to it?"

"Don't worry. It's still out there. Father kept it for you, and let two of the sailors live, as well. We will have a way to other lands."

"We?"

She kissed him again. It tingled on his lips. Did he taste snake? A faint musk?

"Never fear," she murmured. "I'm fond of you, Fool Wolf, but I'm not going attached to you, in hopes of a husband and children. That isn't what I want. But I will see more of the world. I've become bored with this island." She scratched him behind the ear. "Anyway. I think you will need my help for a little while, yes?"

"I won't argue with an offer like that," Fool Wolf told her, smiling.

All in all, it seemed the best idea to agree with everything she said, at least until he could walk again.

SLEEPING TIDE

The Hounds of Ash
Part One: The Sleeping Tide

"WHERE ARE WE?" Fool Wolf asked.

He faced darkness, and his fingers gripped cold stone. From somewhere behind him, torchlight cast an inconstant copper glow on the woman crouched at his side. He could make out the gleaming curve of her thigh, the sleek muscles of her back, and enough of her fine-featured face to recognize her.

"Inah?" Fool Wolf said, more insistently. "Where are we?"

"Quiet!" she whispered.

In that wherever place behind them, several men began shouting. Their voices reverberated, as if in a cave.

Which made sense, given the darkness and the stone.

"Wonderful," Inah said. Even in the dim light, her eyes were an impossibly pale jade. "Now suddenly you can talk, just when I don't need you to. Now we'll have to jump."

"Jump? Jump where?"

"Straight out there. Are you ready?"

"No! What's going on?"

For answer she snorted and stood. Something fast, small, and hard clipped the stone next to Fool Wolf's hand, and the shouting took on a triumphant tone.

"Jump or die," she said. She took four steps back, then charged into empty space. Fool Wolf, cursing, leapt with her.

"How far down is it?" he asked, as they hurled into cool black air.

"I have no idea," Inah shouted back.

92

In Fool Wolf's soul, the goddess Chugaachik stirred sleepily, then roared awake.

Where are we? she snarled.

That shocked Fool Wolf more than the fall, which after three heartbeats still hadn't ended.

✠ ✠ ✠

But after the sixth heartbeat something slapped the soles of Fool Wolf's feet so hard it jolted all the way to the top of his skull, filling it with flashes of fire and nonsense. Blood-warm water took him in, and it felt so pleasant and comfortable he thought he would just rest there for awhile.

Rest was denied him, however. Thick, muscular tentacles wrapped around his torso and squeezed. He beat feebly at them, but it was like fighting a tide. Water rushed by, faster and faster, and then his lungs began to ache, and he wondered how the sea would feel when he finally drew a breath.

Then he and his captor burst through the skin of the sea, and he gulped air that tasted of iodine and sewage. So grateful was he for the breath, it took a few moments to start worrying about what had grabbed him, and what had happened to Inah. He pushed again at the tentacles, wishing he had a sword or even a knife — wondering where they were. Wishing he could at least see.

Then he felt sand beneath his back, and the ropy limbs holding him uncoiled, and he lay on a pebbly beach, gasping.

"Inah!" He croaked, after a moment.

"Right here," she answered, from just behind him.

He turned, and realized that he could see her, barely, in a pearly light filtering in from his right. Her naked limbs shone pale.

"Did you —" he began, but then decided he didn't want to know. He and Inah were lovers, companions, partners in crime. He knew she wasn't fully human — she was the daughter of the Tattooed Python King, the god of an island now far distant. If he had been dragged to safety by creatures she somehow commanded, that was one thing.

If those tentacles belonged to her, he simply didn't want to know.

"We should go," Inah said "There's probably an easier way down. The priests may come after us."

"What priests? What are you talking about?"

"You really don't know?"

"I —" Inah didn't know about Chugaachik yet. "No," he finished.

"You got up in the middle of the night. You — come on, there's light this way. We can talk while we walk. But quietly — maybe they'll think we're dead."

She rose and started toward the light.

"Are we still in Pethvang, at least?" Fool Wolf whispered.

"We're in the temple mountain near it. The place where the pilgrims go."

"I crossed the water in my sleep?"

"Yes, on the floating causeway. It took me nearly all night to find you. You were trying to sneak into one of the shrines. You didn't answer me when I tried talking to you. It was like you were still asleep. I had to drag you as far as I got you when you woke up." She turned on him, her face shadowed. "You really — you really don't know any of this?"

"No." But I know someone who does, he thought. "Chugaachik."

"What was that?"

Fool Wolf hadn't realized he had spoken aloud.

"Chugaachik," he repeated.

"Is that a sneeze?"

"No," he said, reluctantly deciding it was time to tell her — because something was wrong. He always remembered what he did when Chugaachik took control. It was part of the curse. "It's the name of a goddess. My totem goddess. She lives in my chest, in my mansion of bone."

"I sensed something like that," Inah murmured. "I can see something in there. Why didn't you tell me? Can she help us escape?"

Fool Wolf laughed bitterly. "She's probably the one who got us in trouble."

Not so, Chugaachik whispered in his ear. *I'm as puzzled as you. Or is this some trick of yours to be rid of me?*

Fool Wolf ignored the goddess. Only he could hear her, anyway. "Chugaachik is a liar," he told Inah. "If I use her power, the price is that she takes control of my body. Then she does very unpleasant things."

"Such as?"

"She killed my cousin."

Your lover, Chugaachik added, in gleeful tones.

"I called on her to save you and your father from Prince Fa, but I was so badly hurt she couldn't make me do anything. If I hadn't been injured, she would have made me kill you."

Oh, we would have done many things before we got to that. Amusing things. Wonderful things. Flashes of bare flesh and blood came with the words. Chugaachik had an inventive imagination.

"She would have *tried* to kill me," Inah corrected. "I am not as easy to murder as you might think."

"She is a very powerful goddess."

And your woman is very sweet meat. Let us show her what we can do.

Inah stopped walking and put her hands on her hips. "And yet you didn't mention this to me? That I might be in danger from my own lover?"

"Chugaachik been weak since the fight on your island," Fool Wolf said. "And I never intend to use her power again."

"And yet you seem to think she set you walking last night. Did you make use of her? When? In our lovemaking, perhaps?"

"No," he grinned, pushing on. Up ahead, a circle of daylight appeared, and now he could make out her face plainly. "That was my own natural stamina."

"And she has never taken control of you in your sleep before?"

"Never. She can't."

No, curse you. If I could, I would do it every night.

"Maybe she can now," Inah said.

Fool Wolf considered that for a long moment. "I didn't kill anyone, torture any children, rape any old women?"

"No. You were very calm."

"That's not like her. Not like her at all."

"Well. Either you are lying to me — not for the first time — or your goddess has changed, somehow. Or we have a great mystery before us." She shrugged, as if it didn't matter which. "Here's more for you to think about. One of the men with the priests recognized you. He shouted your name."

"Really?"

"Yes. Have you ever been to Pethvang before?"

"I've never been to this miserable city in my life," Fool Wolf said, "much less this temple-mountain. I wouldn't be here now if our ship hadn't wrecked up the coast."

"So you say."

Fool Wolf spun her around by the shoulder. "You wanted to come along with me and see the world, remember?"

She stopped, took his face in her hands, and kissed him. "I don't regret it yet," she said, softly. "If you keep talking, I may."

The buttery light of the sun was bright enough to squint at, now. "Before we jumped — how did you know there would be water down here?" Fool Wolf asked.

"I smelled it," she said. "I know about islands. This one is made of soft white stone. Water eats is easily. You remember it? Tall, and flat topped, with nearly sheer sides?"

"Like your own island."

"But mine is of hard, black stone. This one is different. Rain has burrowed wormholes in it, and the tide has chewed into its roots. The two watergods meet in the middle, and gnaw a hollow womb. That is what we jumped into. I smelled the sea, I knew it was there. Look, see there? The shore. The seagods made this tunnel. At high tide, it's probably full of water. We're lucky."

"I didn't think you visited any islands but your own, until you left with me."

"I never did. But my father was a creator of islands, in the ancient days. He told me all about them."

"Is this how we came in, through one of these tunnels?"

"No. There are steps carved on the outside of the island. They go all of the way to the top. That's how the Pilgrims enter — all the way to the top, then halfway back down to the shrine caves. I don't understand why they don't come in this way. It would be easier."

"Because they're pilgrims," Fool Wolf explained. "They always do things the hardest way possible."

"Why?" Inah asked. She knew little of the world of Human Beings.

"I don't know," Fool Wolf answered, honestly.

After a moment they emerged from the tunnel onto a sunlit beach. The sheer monolith of the temple mountain rose above them, a few scraggly trees clinging to its steep sides. The beach graded into a marsh of rushes and waving cattails, and beyond that, perhaps a league away, the city of Pethvang floated.

"This man who recognized me — What did he look like?"

"Very dark skinned, but with red hair. Big, very muscular. Tattoos on his forehead. He had the largest sword I've ever seen."

"You speak literally?" Fool Wolf asked, with faint sarcasm.

She blinked uncomprehendingly. "'Sword' is the word, yes, for the giant metal knives?"

"Yes."

Her description sounded familiar, suddenly. He had seen such a man before.

She must have noticed it on his face. "You know him?"

"Maybe." Fool Wolf surveyed the marsh. "Now we need a boat."

"We're going back to Pethvang?"

"Everything we own is there. It's a big place, full of pilgrims. I doubt the priests can mount a search large enough to find us anytime soon."

"A man is coming," Inah murmured. "Maybe he has a boat."

Fool Wolf looked around. He neither saw nor heard anyone.

"I suppose you smell him?"

Inah stuck out her tongue and waggled it. "I taste him," she replied.

✠ ✠ ✠

They came across an oyster-fisherman a few moments later, a slight, grizzled old man who eyed Inah greedily. He agreed to take them across the inlet to Pethvang for no cost.

"Just so long as the lady doesn't mind me looking at her," he said. "One doesn't see such beauty uncovered often. It is forbidden." He pulled on the oars a few times. "How did you come to be on the temple-mountain? And how without clothes? Are you pilgrims?"

"We were shipwrecked," Fool Wolf said. "We lost everything."

"Well, Thesk-of-the-Sea must have smiled on you, to bring you to Pethvang. It's the greatest city in the world."

"It certainly is," Fool Wolf lied, glancing at the motley collection of dilapidated houseboats and stilt-dwellings they were approaching. The central city beyond, with its slender towers and colonnaded piazzas was grander, but Fool Wolf had seen Lhe, Nhol, Rumq Qaj. "Why did they build the city in the water?"

"Ah! It was an arrangement we made with Thesk-of-the-sea, long ago. We once lived on the mainland, but the marauding Reng tribes were troublesome. Thesk offered us haven. He took the tide out for eight and fifty days, long enough for our ancestors to lay the foundations of the Quays."

"And what do you give Thesk in return?"

"Why, our love, of course, and our respect."

"So Pethvang doesn't really float," Inah said. "It's built on stone."

"Such music, your voice!" the fisherman exclaimed, his gaze fixed on her breasts. "Most of it floats. The Quays are the only solid part of the city. The rest of Pethvang was built on barges. You'll see that, when you're there. The Quays stay level — the rest of the city goes up and down with the tide."

Fool Wolf and Inah had already spent a night in Pethvang — or part of one, anyway — but he hadn't noticed that. He reflected that the barges must be very large indeed.

"What's your name?" Inah asked the man.

"Ner. Ner Mank."

"Ner Mank, is there someplace we can get clothes? At one of these stilt-houses, perhaps?" She reached over absently and rubbed the fisherman's nearly bald head.

He blushed a darker shade of bronze. "I think we can manage that," he said.

✢ ✢ ✢

For an embrace and a kiss on the cheek from Inah, Ner took them beneath a clothesline, where they stole a loincloth for Fool Wolf and a sarong for Inah. Then the old fisherman paddled them into a long canal marked on each side by towering statues carved of the same white stone as the temple mountain. The first they passed looked new, sharply carved men and women bearing batons in the shape of a paddle in one hand and conch shells in the other. As they moved into the city, the statues became progressively more weathered, until they were nothing more than vaguely human-shaped stones.

"Your kings and queens?" Inah asked.

"No. Those are the sacred heroes, the ones who battle Thesk-of-the-Wave."

"I thought Thesk was kindly to you."

"That's Thesk-of-the-Sea. Of course, both Thesks are the same god, I suppose, just as the dark moon and the bright moon are the same goddess. But how different they are in different aspects. Now, see! Here are the Quays."

They had been passing through the city for some time. On either side of the corridor formed by the statues, buildings crowded together on what Fool Wolf could now see were numerous barges, some of moderate size, some massive enough to place a small town on. They were connected by bridges and heavy timbers. But the waterway now entered the horseshoe-shaped harbor in the very center of the city. Each side of the horseshoe was perhaps half a league in length.

Fool Wolf had first seen Pethvang at high tide, and had besides been exhausted from the shipwreck and the effort of relieving a pair of would-be pirates of their longboat and jade coins. Then, the water had come to the very lip of the fitted-stone walkways of that outlined the harbor. Now the Quays stood the length of two men out of the water, revealing their barnacle-encrusted sides. Along the inside — the harbor side — a thousand watercraft were docked; double-hulled merchantmen from the Land of Nine Princes, battered twelve-oared galleys from Lhe, lateen-rigged phanga from the Jara archipelago, princely yachts, and leaky fishing canoes like the one they were in. The Quays themselves had broad backs, and a few strides from the waterfront the soaring spires and gilded domes of palaces and public buildings challenged the sky.

The rest of the city — which stretched leagues in each direction — had sunken since Fool Wolf had last seen it, though parts of it were no less grand than the Quays. At high tide, the tallest towers on the barges had been higher than the tallest towers on the stone heart of the city. Each day, one part of the city eclipsed the other in stature.

Ner Mank put them off on a landing, and with a final wave and leer at Inah, went to sell his oysters. Fool Wolf and Inah warily wound their uncertain way to the inn where they had taken lodging the day before.

The attendant, a round man with round eyes, met Fool Wolf and Inah at the door.

"Good day, lord and lady," he said, bowing jerkily. "I did not see you go out. How can we attend you?"

"An aquaintance of mine was to drop by. Has he come asking for me?"

"Not to my knowledge, lord."

Fool Wolf affected an exaggerated sigh. "Very well. Have some wine and an evening meal sent up to my room."

When they were back in their room, Fool Wolf confirmed that the jade coins he had hidden under a floor board were still there. The curved Banwan sword he had taken from the pirates and his clothes hadn't been disturbed either.

"Is it safe to stay here?" Inah asked.

Fool Wolf shrugged. "It depends on what they thought we were doing, whether they know we survived, and how efficient their city guard is. In my experience, in a city this large, with as many inns as it has, we have time for a meal, at least. They've probably given up the search."

"But the man who recognized you. What of him?"

At that moment, someone rapped on the door. It was a serving girl, bearing platters of seared tuna, pickled squid and a pale yellow pudding she called ithel.

"You'll have a good view from the balcony," she said, cheerfully. Fool Wolf barely heard her — he was starving.

Inah and Fool Wolf sat on their balcony, eating, watching the sun set and the city rise. Inah went back over the details of Fool Wolf's behavior the night before, but they made no more progress on deciphering the mystery.

As the city lay beneath the last red gasps of the sun, Fool Wolf heard music approaching, and a crowd began to gather along the boulevard below their window.

"A good view of what?" Fool Wolf said. He'd been so preoccupied with hunger he thought the serving girl meant the sunset, or the city.

Pethvang shook to drumming, conch shell trumpets, and wailing reedy pipes. The already colorful crowd below become positively fluorescent as hordes of children arrived, bearing great baskets of flowers. The throng took the blooms, waving them high as the drumming came nearer.

A bizarre parade followed. The drums were wider than the length of a horse, mounted on carriages dragged by twenty men each. The trumpet players and pipers followed, and then a long procession of dancers in grotesque masks that covered their entire bodies. Men and women — some painted all black, others all white — tripped odd, drunken dances. Giant crocodiles and sea snakes of wood, leather, and paper wriggled down the streets, some with as many as twelve people in them.

After that came the boats. Canoes and catamarans, lap planked barques, sleek warships with iron prows shaped like sharks heads, all dragged on wheeled frames.

It was quite a spectacle, but Fool Wolf was growing bored with it. Inah seemed delighted, however, and he continued to watch with her.

After the boats, warriors in cuirasses of lacquered crocodile skin and brightly colored headwraps flourished swords, spears, and bows, shouting fiercely. Finally, following them, a palanquin so huge it took thirty groaning men to bear it came through, and the crowd frenzied, tossing their flowers. The seat of the litter was high and flat, clearly a replica of the temple mountain, and on it stood one lone figure, holding a baton shaped like a paddle in one hand and a conch-shell in the other. He had red hair, and in the fading light his skin appeared as black as pitch. On his back was sheathed a sword almost as long as he was tall.

Fool Wolf ducked back into the shadows of his room, Inah one step behind him.

"That was the man!" she exclaimed. "The one who knew you in the temple!" She shook the back of her palm at Fool Wolf. "And you do know him!"

"We've met," Fool Wolf allowed. "His name is Uzhdon, the Opal of Nah."

"You met," she said, skeptically. "Does he have an argument with you?"

"I threw him out of the window of a very high tower." He scratched his chin. "Twice."

"And he lived?"

"That sword on his back is a godsword. It will only allow him to be killed in fair combat."

"And you weren't fighting him?"

"Not exactly. I just distracted him and threw him out the window."

"Twice."

"It's a long story."

"So Uzhdon has little love for you."

"I believe he has sworn to hunt me down and kill me," Fool Wolf admitted.

"He seems to be the champion of these people, the sort they make the statues of."

"Yes, he does, doesn't he?" Fool Wolf furrowed his brow.
"But he told me he was from Nah."
"Where is that?"
"Three months travel from here, at least."
"Maybe he lied."
Fool Wolf chuckled. "That's very unlikely."
"Well — could he have anything to do with your sleep-
walking?"
Fool Wolf had already thought of that. "I don't know.
Maybe."
Yes, Chugaachik said. It must be him. Follow him. Kill
him.
"Let's get some rest," Fool Wolf suggested, ignoring his
goddess. "Tomorrow, first light, we leave Pethvang."
"And if you walk in your sleep again?"
"Stop me."
"Shall a tie you up?"
"That sounds fun, but no. Still, speaking of fun . . . ."
They tangled, squirmed, and sweated. Surrounded by
the sent of Inah's faint, snaky musk, Fool Wolf drifted off
to sleep.
And in his sleep, it seemed, he slipped below the lake,
whose surface is the world most men know. He drifted
down, a sinking leaf.
His feet touched upon gray stone, a plain that stretched
away to jagged peaks in very direction. Two of them exhaled plumes of dark ash. He walked, and after a time came
to a city of the same stone. Flanking the broad way were
twin statues, crouching figures of jackal-headed lions beside
which Fool Wolf was ant-sized. Their eyes gleamed like
fishscales, and the sight of them brought blood to his loins
and jolted a fierce anger through him. He laughed,
Chugaachik's laugh. Beyond the statues, the city was
massive cubes and columns, and a thousand thousand
kneeling men and women in rags. They seemed to be
chanting a hymn as gray dust from the sky settled on their
shoulders.
And something parted the crowd in the distance, a man
in the mask of a black-beaked bird. A darkly patterned kilt

his only clothing, his flesh was so white it seemed to shine. The crowd shouted a name to him, but Fool Wolf could not make it out. The masked man came on, white light blazing through the eyeholes of his mask, until he stood directly in front of Fool Wolf.

In one hand the masked figure held the leashes of four hounds, or what Fool Wolf first took for hounds. One was as white as his master, so gaunt as to be almost skeletal, with sapphire eyes. The next was more tiger than dog, hunch-shouldered like the grass bears of Fool Wolf's native steppes. The third, sleek and gray, had the head of a hawk, and the fourth was a black, squirming mass that might have been made of worms.

Now Fool Wolf wanted to run, but his feet were rooted. The Earth began to tremble, and the hounds drew so near the stench of their breath made him want to vomit.

The masked figure halted, regarded him for a long moment, then removed his mask.

The face was so magnificent Fool Wolf wanted to weep, and he feared the beauty was so terrible he would die from the mere sight of it. But then the face changed, became dusky, with red hair and curling tattoos on its forehead. Became Uzhdon, the Opal of Nah.

"Come," Uzhdon said. "Come."

✠ ✠ ✠

Fool Wolf woke pinned by some heavy weight, both arms twisted behind his back and held by something that cut into his wrists like steel jaws.

"What?" he managed.

"Are you awake?" Inah's voice came, from above him.

"Yes! Let me go!"

"Who am I?" she demanded.

"You are Inah, the Python King's daughter. I met you on the island of Ranga Lehau."

"Very well." The pressure vanished, and his wrists were released. He scrambled to his feet.

"What happened?"

"You fell asleep. You started to walk again."

He shivered. "We're leaving this city. Now."

"Fool Wolf?"

"Yes?"

"When our ship was wrecked on the rocks up the coast, I was asleep. You were at the tiller."

"Yes."

"Were you awake?"

"Yes," Fool Wolf lied. In fact, he had fallen asleep and awakened to the sound of rocks clashing against the hull, but had never seen the point in admitting that to Inah. He still didn't.

"Then you think it is a coincidence that your friend Uzhdon is here?"

"It must be. He must have seen me and done some sort of sorcery."

"Why? Why not simply come kill you?"

"I don't know and I don't care. Maybe he's afraid I will throw him from a window again. I'm leaving, now. you can come with me or not."

"Of course I'm coming with you, you fool."

They stole a boat and made the mainland by morning, slipping through the Reng forests in the early light. By that night they were entering the highlands, following a steep path that wound past stone shrines decorated with human skulls. Near sundown they came to a prospect from which they could see the bay, Pethvang, and the temple mountain looming over it. They camped farther up, where the curve of a ridge obscured the view.

Once more, Fool Wolf awoke pinioned.

The next day they reached a high plateau. They bargained for food at a Reng hunting camp, crossed the escarpment, and began descending into the valley that the Reng called Sleeping Mother.

And the next morning, Fool Wolf awoke in Inah's sure grip. This time he had escaped her long enough to run all the way back up to the plateau.

Three days later, cursing Uzhdon, Uzhdon's mother, Nah, and Pethvang, Fool Wolf and Inah gave up and returned to the floating city, seeking the Opal of Nah, and an answer.

✝ ✝ ✝

Fool Wolf woke with his wrists tied tightly behind his back. For a few awful moments, he didn't know what was going on, but then he realized that Inah was beside him, stroking his forehead, soothing him. He smelled brine.

"Shhh," she said. "It worked."

"Untie me!" He had agreed to be tied, this time, to make it easier for her. But he didn't like it.

The bonds parted, and Fool Wolf rubbed his aching wrists. His skin was rough and salty. "I'm becoming very tired of asking 'where are we?'," He muttered. "Are we in the temple mountain?"

"No," Inah said. "You went into the city, to the eastern-most point of it, then leapt into the sea. I had to save you from drowning."

"Were we wrong, then? Uzhdon is not drawing me to him?"

"We weren't wrong. Uzhdon is here."

"Which is where?" He looked around him. They were in a large chamber of cut and polished coral. The walls were incised, floor to ceiling, with some sort of script. A raised altar and a large, half-carved statue occupied one end of the chamber. Though unfinished, Fool Wolf was certain he could see a resemblance to Uzhdon in it.

"Below Pethvang," Inah said.

"Below?"

"Yes. The quays are built on a coral reef. The reef has caves in it. I believe Uzhdon is in a cave below this one, and I sense the easiest way to it is through here."

"How do you know he's down there?"

Her eyes flickered uncertainly. "I feel something," she replied.

Fool Wolf frowned, but let that pass. "How long have we been here?" He asked.

"A few moments. I did not think it was a good idea to confront Uzhdon with you in your sleeping state."

"Good thinking. Let's find the entrance before —"

"Not just yet," someone else said.

Filing into the other end of the shrine were several men in parrot-feather robes, and perhaps twenty armored warriors.

The man who had spoken was one of the robe-clad men, a stocky, flat-faced fellow with broad nostrils. He waved the back of his hand at Fool Wolf and narrowed his eyes.

"You were the ones we saw before, in the temple mountain. The ones who tried to spoil the inaman ceremony. Now you seek to desecrate the pae shrine of Thesk-of-the-Sea. Why?"

"We weren't trying to desecrate anything," Inah said. "My friend is afflicted with a curse that drew him here."

"Really?" the priest sniffed. "And it drew him to the temple mountain as well?"

Fool Wolf placed a hand on Inah's shoulder. "My friend speaks half the truth," he said. "I am cursed, that is true. I healer put a song on me that would take me to the cure. I believe it has been leading me to your champion."

"He was in the Temple Mountain that night," Inah added. "And he is here, yes?"

"In a manner of speaking," the priest replied. "If your intentions were innocent, why did you flee in the temple mountain?"

"We were chased," Fool Wolf replied, simply. "We realized we must have accidentally violated some tapu unknown to us, and became fearful of the punishment."

"Well, you are fortunate. You did not actually interrupt the inaman ceremony, and so no harm was done. And this shrine has been rendered unsacred until the champion has completed his task of battling Thesk-of-the-Waves."

"When will that be?"

"Today, at high tide. He has been battling Thesk for four days, now, and that is the time allotted in the founding times, when Thesk-of-the-Sea took the tide out for us. Thesk-of-the-Waves demanded a contest with a champion, every ten years."

"And when he is done fighting, we can see him? What if he loses?"

"Win or lose, it doesn't matter to Thesk, so long as he has a battle. But you can see the champion now, if you wish. You can watch him battle. We men of Pethvang cannot — it is tapu for us — but you are foreigners."

"Will Thesk attack us?" Inah asked.

"Assuredly not. He demands one — and only one — champion every ten years." The priest shrugged. "If you wish to see him, the way lies behind the altar. You may borrow an oil lamp. If not, you may remain here and pray, or leave. It is up to you. But make no noise, nor disturb our meditations. Count yourself lucky that your ignorance did not lead you into real trouble."

"Thank you," Inah said.

The priests nodded, then went back out the way they came, the warriors close on their heels.

Fool Wolf and Inah found the passage behind the altar, two large valves of coral set into the floor. They were too heavy to lift, but a windlass on the wall proved the mechanism to open them. What lay beneath was a steep stairway going down, smelling of the sea.

Fool Wolf walked down a few steps, Inah behind him. After a few more, she tapped him on the shoulder.

"The tide comes this high," she said, indicating the stairwell, a fingersbreadth below the valves.

"What do you mean?"

"I mean at high tide, this stairwell fills all of the way up."

"Horse Mother!" Fool Wolf cried, bolting back up the steps.

If he had made it up another heads-length, the slamming valve would have broken his neck. The echo hummed down the stairs and back up. He pushed at the portal, but it didn't budge.

"Well," Inah said. "This wasn't very clever at all."

"It was your idea," Fool Wolf reminded her. He pushed again at the valve. "Well," he said. "I wonder if Uzhdon is even down here."

"He is, or was," Inah replied. "I taste him."
"Well. Let's follow your tongue, then," Fool Wolf replied. "If it's never brought me luck, it's a least brought me pleasure."

They found Uzhdon in a rough twin of the shrine above, a large chamber with an alter. This one was crusted with slime, seaweed, and pale, purplish barnacles, and there was a large pool of water in the middle of it. Uzhdon turned to look at them as they descended the stairs.
"The four days are passed?" Uzhdon asked. His voice sounded strange, as if something was trying to strangle him.
"As you see, I am not the champion that you —" he stopped, staring at Fool Wolf's face.
"You aren't a priest," Uzhdon said. "I remember you."
Fool Wolf said nothing, but the hairs on the back of his neck, crusted as they were with brine, nevertheless stood on end.
Uzhdon, the Opal of Nah, was seated on a raised dais. He was chained to it by enormous links of coral, his hands and feet hidden by massive manacles of the same substance. The man himself looked haggard and waterlogged, though his eyes still retained a bright gleam.
"Yes," Uzhdon continued, slowly. "I know you! You threw me out of a window in Rumq Qaj!" He frowned. "Twice! And the second time the whole building fell on me."
"Well, you were planning to kill me," Fool Wolf reminded him.
"In fair combat!" Uzhdon shifted his gaze to Inah. "Lady, I advise you against associating with this man. He is without honor or scruples, and a terrible goddess lives in his breast."
"I'm aware of all that," Inah replied.
"Well, I'm sure you must not know him as well as you think," Uzhdon went on, "or you would not be with him. I sense nothing evil about you, though I do see you have some godblood in you. I urge you to free me —" he broke

off, and a look of suspicion crossed his face. "Is this your doing, Fool Wolf? Did you send the dreams, and the spirit that brought me sleep-walking to this place?"

"Oh, great gods of the mountain," Fool Wolf groaned, sinking down onto a damp coral step.

"Well?" Uzhdon said. "Can't you at least tell me why you bewitched me?"

"Who chained you down here, Uzhdon?"

The warrior looked puzzled. "Why, the priests, of course. You must know that. They want me to fight their god, Thesk."

"How can you fight a god, chained like that?"

"I'm supposed to fight him in the netherworld, after I've drowned. The tide fills this chamber, I'm supposed to die, then fight their god in spirit form. If I defeat him, they make a statue for my soul to live in."

"You agreed to do this?"

Uzhdon pursed his lips. "Well, they didn't tell me everything, at first. They led me to understand Thesk-of-the-Waves was evil, and as you know, my mission is to destroy evil, as I did at Rumq Qaj."

"When did they tell you you would have to die?"

"After they put the chains on."

"You aren't very smart, Opal of Nah."

"I'm perhaps too trusting. After all, I trusted you, and you betrayed me. But cynicism is the first of many steps to damnation." He suddenly looked upset. "Do I understand by your questions that you had nothing to do with summoning me here?"

"Why in the name of the Horse Mother would I do that?" Fool Wolf asked. "I hoped never to see you again."

"Then please accept my apologies. I accused you without reason." Uzhdon paused. "Why are you here, if I may ask?"

"He thought you were summoning him," Inah said.

"Hush!" Fool Wolf snapped. "Don't tell him anything he doesn't need to know."

"What? Then we were both tricked?"

"No," Fool Wolf said. "You were tricked. I was enspelled."

"But by who?" Inah asked. "For what reason?"

"Do you also dream of a city?" Uzhdon asked. "A city in a wasteland, and a man with the face of a hawk coursing four hounds?"

Fool Wolf bit his lip, but did not answer that question. Instead he pointed up. "The priests think you've been dead for four days, battling their god."

"Yes, but of course Hukop, my sword, brother to my totem, will only allow me to die in even combat."

"So the tide comes in, and you just sit there, underwater."

"It is very unpleasant," Uzhdon acknowledged.

"What happens if no one fights Thesk?" Fool Wolf wondered.

"If Thesk is anything like my father," Inah said, "he will not take lightly to his covenant being broken. I do not think we will want to be in Pethvang when the tide rises." She pointed to the pool in the center of the floor, which was larger than it had been when the conversation began. "And it's rising now."

"Will that pool take us out?"

"It certainly goes to the sea. That's probably why you jumped in, earlier. More than that I cannot say." She shifted. "I can swim for a great distance without air. But you —"

"Can you find out how far it is?"

"Yes."

He leaned over and kissed her. "Good luck."

She smiled and dove into the pool.

After she left, a silence settled between Uzhdon and Fool Wolf. The warrior broke it.

"You're not going to free me, are you?" Uzhdon asked.

"Why should I?" Fool Wolf replied. "So you can kill me as soon as you get the chance?"

"You have evil in you," Uzhdon said, reasonably.

"There you have your answer."

Uzhdon drew himself up. "Suppose I promise not to kill you until after this is over?"

"Until what is over?"

"Until we discover who has bespelled the two of us and dealt with them. And even then I will give you fair warning, and a day's start."

"A week's start," Fool Wolf amended.

"Very well. One week of seven days, from morning to morning. I swear it by my ancestors, by the covenant of Nah-hatham, and by my totem, the Seven-Bearded Hawk, the Fourth Thunderbolt."

"Fine."

"But will you swear in turn not to throw me from windows, cliffs, or ledges, or to take me unawares in any manner while our truce lasts?"

"Why of course," Fool Wolf said. "By my people, the Mang, I swear it." His people had never really cared much for him, anyway.

"Good. Can you free me of these, then?"

It was Fool Wolf's lock-picking tools that eventually got him through the shackles, and then Uzhdon rose to his impressive full height.

"Thank you," he said. "Though you only serve your self-interest, I commend you. You have done a good thing, no matter how inadvertently."

At that moment, Inah came up from the pool.

She took in the new situation quickly.

"You might make it," she said. "I can't be sure."

"I don't like the sound of that," Fool Wolf said.

"I can swim it," Uzhdon said. "My sword will not let me drown."

"And so?"

"The priests, I have determined, are evil. I shall swim above and slay them."

"I'll help," Inah added.

"No, lady," Uzhdon said. "The risk is too great. I would not jeopardize such beauty."

Did Inah blush, and bow her head a bit? Fool Wolf felt a sudden flash of — of, well, something. Surely Inah did not in any way admire this fool.

"There must be another way," Fool Wolf said.

The floor was covered in water now, and the level was rising all too swiftly.

"There is not," Uzhdon replied. "You have freed me; we have made a bargain." He turned, and leapt into the water.

Inah hesitated. "Will he keep his bargain?"

"Yes," Fool Wolf said. "Every word of it. Go help him."

She hesitated, then kissed him again. He savored the taste.

"Go," he said. "I'll see you above."

She nodded, and plunged into the rising waters.

✠ ✠ ✠

They aren't coming back, Chugaachik sneered.

Fool Wolf had moved to the top of the stairs, just beneath the sealed trapdoor. The lantern sat beside him as he watched the water rise.

"I know," he replied.

You know?

"I listened very carefully to Uzhdon's promise. He never promised to open the valves and free me. If he meant to free me, he would have said so. He promised not to kill me himself, and he won't, but he won't object to the water doing it. And Inah . . ." that part was just a feeling, but he trusted it.

If you knew that, why didn't you make him promise to free you?

"I don't want him to."

Then why didn't you go with them? You might have made it, with your snake-woman's help.

"Because I wanted to talk to you. I'm about to die. This is the time you start raging about how I ought to release you, how you'll save me, and how much I'll enjoy your perverse antics in my body. But you haven't said a thing."

The goddess was silent, but she moved within him, brushing his thoughts with a sleekness like fur and warm flesh, a scent like burning anise, a hunger that only an immortal could know.

"You've closed wounds on me that would have bled ten men to death," Fool Wolf went on. "We bit through the neck of a giant together. Maybe we couldn't break these doors, but you could give me the strength to swim after Uzhdon and Inah, couldn't you?"

Again, she was silent. The water crept higher.

"It's you being summoned, Chugaachik, not me. You. You just happen to be in my body."

Nonsense.

"No, not nonsense. The priest in Rumq Qaj was able to free you without my consent. Now someone is controlling you without my consent, and when I'm asleep, they allow you the use of my limbs. But it isn't your will being done, it's theirs."

You're guessing.

"So are you, but we've guessed the same thing. And now your afraid to take control of me when I'm awake because your afraid that will strengthen whoever-it-is' power over you."

"No."

"Where are your promises, then, your cajoling, your taunts? You don't want to entice me with the pleasures we will have together, once you've helped me escape from here?" The water had touched his toes, now. With it came a tingle that went straight to his head, a feeling of being crushed, buried alive. His throat went dry and his fingers trembled a bit.

Darken your mouth.

Fool Wolf put his back to the portal and heaved until he thought his back would break. The air was getting stale.

Before the air could go too bad, he took four deep, slow breaths, holding the last, dropped the lantern down the stair, and dove.

The lantern sputtered fitfully for a heartbeat or two, and the water-filled way was green, almost tranquil. Then the light went out, and he swam through the darkness before the world was born.

Down, down. Before he even reached the lower temple, his lungs began to hurt.

Come, he said. Come, Chugaachik.

No.

You don't have a choice. I've never compelled you because I've never wanted you in me. But I have the right.

No.

Come.

His eyes suddenly blazed with a different sort of vision, and strength went like black wine into his veins. The world was limned in shades of blue and gold, the void of cold stone, the glistening heartstrands in living things. He swam down through the pool at the bottom of the shrine, through the twisting tunnels of coral, toward the sea beyond. All pain was forgotten, all remorse snuffed out. There was only anger, and a faint taste like fear.

✝ ✝ ✝

He emerged from the water like a two legged shark, smelling blood, and thought fled him as he lunged forward at the first prey he saw. His talons tore soft flesh, and blood sprayed like surf. The air was already full of incoherent shrieking, but more immediate screams went up around him. He reached for the next person — a young woman, perhaps sixteen, and his lips curved up in delight. He held her up before her, laughing at her fear, thirsting . . .

No, Chugaachik said. No. He will find us, like this.

An image lept up like a flame — the city, the hawk-masked man, the hounds. He is reaching — Hide me, Fool Wolf. Lock me away. And do not sleep.

The rage leaked out of him reluctantly, so reluctantly that the girl nearly died, anyway. But finally he put her down, gazed dully at the messy ruin of the priest at his feet, and tried to understand what was going on around him.

Do not sleep. And then Chugaachik was silent, burrowed as deeply in his Mansion of Bone as she could go.

He had come up, not on one of the stable, stone Quays, but on one of the huge barges that supported the rest of the city. It was tilted a bit, so that he had a hard time standing up straight.

The reason he had not come up on a Quay was obvious
— they were underwater, and even the tallest towers upon
them were half submerged. The air was filled with the
sound of beams shattering, iron twisting and snapping
as the barges tried to tear free of the bridges and walks
that chained them to the city's rocky heart. One of the largest barges had already tilted nearly vertically, tumbling
its occupants into water already boiling with thrashing
human beings. Houses and temples crumbled and slid
into the deep. Other, luckier barges at the periphery of
the city seemed to have broken free — or more likely been
severed— and were floating away on the impossibly high
tide.

Never trust a god. If Thesk could take the tide away
so Pethvang could be built, it was certainly logical that
he could make it rise to destroy the city. And anything
a god could do, he would do, given time and the proper
childish fit of pique.

The floor beneath Fool Wolf's feet turned more sharply
sea-and-skyward, and he began to run. A row of buildings
above him suddenly collapsed and slid toward him,
sweeping a handful of people into the sea. Fool Wolf
bounded over the flying rubble, thinking to take back to
the water, but at the edge he hesitated. The sinking barges
were sucking people down in their wakes, and to make
matters worse, he saw the fins of sharks cutting among
the swimmers. No, he would find a boat.

Something tore, and the barge tilted so quickly it was
almost like a catapult. He noted, vaguely, that the upper
towers of the buildings on the quays were crawling with
antlike figures. Then he was in the air, and realized he
was taking his chances with the sharks, after all.

☩ ☩ ☩

He did not sleep. He walked among the dead and
dying on the beach, among the wailing quick. He did not
see Uzhdon or Inah, nor did he expect to. Chugaachik
did not so much as whisper to him.

He did not sleep, but he knew which direction to go. He could feel a path pulsing in him, deep where Chugaachik was buried. The path did not lead back to ruined Pethvang, or to the temple mountain, but away, across the plateau, northwest.

Weary and alone, Fool Wolf turned his feet in that direction.

The Hounds of Ash
Part Two: The Opal of Nah

FOOL WOLF LAY IN A PILE OF DEAD MEN, trying not to gag as a maggot crawled across his lip. The inside of his eyelids had faded from red to black, so he knew the sun had set, but his ears told him the cracked granite plaza surrounding him still swarmed with warriors. Fewer than this morning, when he had first arrived, but enough to kill Fool Wolf if he so much as twitched.

A handful of squirming corpse-eaters spilled on his face as two of the warriors lifted a body from the pile.

"How could this happen?" one of them said. The speaker's boot brushed Fool Wolf's ear. The language he spoke was that of Nah, which differed only a little from the dialects of the mountain tribes Fool Wolf had traveled among for months on his way to this place.

"The end must be upon us, Uteb," another man murmured. "Our greatest hero has turned against us, slaughtered the priests that raised him, and stolen the keys to the gates of the Strictured Land. What else can it mean?"

Hands clamped Fool Wolf's ankles and wrists. He let his body go as lax as possible — the corpses around him had long since lost their after-death stiffness.

They threw him, and he landed in an uncomfortable position, still among corpses.

"At least that one didn't come apart," Uteb said.

"Hurry, you two!" A more distant voice shouted. "The Heroq-rite priest shrove their souls free. If we don't get them to the well by midnight, their spirits will be lost to the Strictured Land. The poor bastards have already had to rot out here for four days."

"How does that matter, anymore?" The warrior nearest Fool Wolf wondered. "The Opal of Nah has sundered the gate. What is a few more souls lost to the Strictured Land next to what will come from that?"

"I don't know, Shelof," Uteb replied. "But they don't tell as everything, the priesthood. The Rector commanded we clear these bodies and kill any strangers near the gate on sight, and that's what I'll do, because if anyone can save us, it's the Lord Rector."

"You think so?" Shelof replied. "Some say his travels abroad infected him with strange ideas."

"Nonsense."

"Really? The great Uzhdon, our priceless Opal, traveled abroad, and see what he has done."

Uteb was silent, after that.

✠ ✠ ✠

A bit later, Fool Wolf discovered he had been moved to a wagon of some sort, for it jolted forward and then rumbled along the roughly paved road he had walked in on.

The drivers weren't Shelof and Uteb, but two other men. After a few moments of chatter, he gathered their names were Izhar and Potek.

"They shouldn't have tried to stand before Uzhdon, the poor bastards," Izhar offered.

"What choice did they have?" Potek replied, in a voice as low and grating as a turning millstone. "The Rector commanded it."

"But Uzhdon can't be slain by superior numbers. He bears the totemsword Hukop. He can only die in fair combat."

"What would you have done to stop him?"

Izhar considered that for a moment. "If all of these men had fought him one at a time, single combat —"

"— they would still be dead," Petok finished. "No swordsman is better than Uzhdon."

"Probably. But Uzhdon would still be fighting, you see? It would have gone slower. It would have given the priests time to think of something."

"Huh. Not a bad idea, that," Petok rumbled.

"But," Izhar said, lowering his voice further, "who is to say Uzhdon should be stopped?"

"He's gone mad, that's why! If he awakes the sleepers in the Strictured land —"

"Uzhdon is our best, our chosen. Only the pure of heart can bear Hukop, after all. Suppose It's Uzhdon who is in the right, and the lord Rector who has gone mad? What did we see, after all? Uzhdon and some foreign princess arrive from the southern mountains. The Rector's men come to greet him. They all vanish into the temple, and then Uzhdon fights his way out. He cuts a path straight to the gate, opens it with the Heroq priesthood key, then seals it behind him."

"As I said," Petok growled, "mad. And he didn't take the sacred book to guide him — he left it in the Heroq-rite chamber. The darkness or the traps may have already killed him."

"Uzhdon can't be killed by traps, either, not if his heart is pure. I think it is, and many of us trust the Opal more than we do the Rector." Izhar's voice dropped even lower. "The Hawk-Totem men are all with Uzhdon. They've sent for his brother, Ilupor."

"For what purpose?"

"There is one more key, held by the Sipost priesthood. But who will they give it to?"

"The Rector, of course," Petok replied. "So he can follow Uzhdon and stop him from waking the First Evil."

"Maybe they will give it to the Rector," Izhar replied, slyly. "Maybe not. When Ilupor arrives, perhaps will we see something different." The cart began to slow.

"Ah. There is the well, ahead, I can see the torches. You did not hear me speak of this, eh Petok?"

"I did not. But what I did not hear, I will nevertheless consider. The Rector has made many enemies."

"They say Ilupor is coming tomorrow evening, on the west road. None will look for him to come from that direction." Izhar's voice changed inflection. "Unless he is betrayed."

"You shouldn't give out secrets to those you aren't sure of," Petok warned. "You need not worry about me, but be careful."

"I am careful, Petok. I know your heart. Only those men most corrupted by the Rector would betray Ilupor. They are few, and easily known."

Fool Wolf didn't know what the well was, exactly, but it didn't sound like something he wanted to be thrown down. Hiding in the corpses had been his only choice when the warriors had arrived, but he was now rather weary of their company.

He rolled from the cart. The soft thump he made when he hit the road wasn't audible over the clattering of wheels on stone, and in the dark he didn't imagine the two men would miss one corpse.

It felt good to move. It would feel better to bath, to scrub off the dried milk of the dead that crusted his skin.

Toward that end he found a swiftly flowing stream, blistering cold, and spent a quarter of the night scouring himself. He found leaves that smelled like eucalyptus when bruised and rubbed a little on the back of his wrist. When no itch developed, he brushed the rest of his body with the leaves.

He sat there, shivering a little, looking up at the stars. He could just make out the Yuchagaage the Hunter, on the horizon. He looked just as he did in the Steppes of the Mang, where Fool Wolf had been born — half a world a way and three tens of summers ago.

Desire prickled along his belly, a sensation like a rough, ghostly tongue flicking, sharp nails scratching at his thighs. He smelled scorched hair, sour wine and smoke-scented flesh.

The goddess that lived in his chest was waking.

We should not be here, Chugaachik purred. Her voice rattled in his chest and behind his ear. No one else could hear it.

"Well, there you are," Fool Wolf remarked. "I haven't heard from you in two full moons. What are you hiding from?"

I do not hide, sweet thing. I crouch, and wait for prey. But I am no fool. I must be cautious. Something is calling me, and I cannot resist it.

"I'm well aware of that. It's my feet you use to walk with, if I'm ever foolish enough to fall asleep without having someone cage me. So why complain about where we are? It's you who brought us here."

You've been walking in daylight, the goddess accused, without being forced. You approach our enemy on purpose.

"Yes. If I follow the call during the day, it lets me sleep at night."

You can't capitulate!

"Believe me, I tried everything I knew," Fool Wolf replied. "But I will not spend the rest of my life tied up like a goat for slaughter every time I need to sleep. So we're going to the source of this summoning, and we'll kill it if we can, and that's that."

You're following the woman, Inah.

"That too," Fool Wolf admitted, remembering Inah's green eyes, the feel of her legs wrapped around him, the scent of her obsidian hair. Inah, who was not quite human herself, who laughed at most of his foolishness. Inah, who was as much as orphan in the world as he was . . .

She betrayed you and left you to die. Chugaachik reminded him She went with Uzhdon, your enemy.

"Maybe she didn't have a choice," Fool Wolf replied. "Maybe she was called, too. Uzhdon certainly was. Something brought us all together and then sent us here."

That makes no sense. What would call all of us?

"You are a goddess. Uzhdon bears a god in his sword. Inah is the daughter of a python-god."

And in our traveling we have passed by, over and under more gods than there are stars in the sky. Where are they?

Fool Wolf shrugged. "You know more about these things than I do."

Where are we?

"In the valley of Nah, Uzhdon's homeland. The call led me to a gate in a mountainside. Uzhdon and Inah already went through, and left a pile of corpses outside. I was trying to figure out how to go through the gate after him when a few hundred warriors showed up, apparently from some outpost a few days march from here. I hid in the corpses." Where does this gate go?

"Someplace they call the Strictured Land."

Yellow light flashed in Fool Wolf's skull, and he saw a desert of bones and a shining masked figure with four hounds walking before him. He felt the sharp, simple terror of a cornered animal.

Then the vision faded.

"You know this place," Fool Wolf said. "What are these dreams I'm having? What will Uzhdon find beyond that gate?"

I don't know.

"Liar."

I might have known once. Something is clouding me.

"Making you stupid, you mean?"

He got no answer to that, other than the sudden sensation of having very sharp teeth, and of wanting to use them on someone.

"Stop that," he said. "I need to think."

My clever sweet has a plan?

"Always. But it may not be a good plan. Let me think. And don't let me sleep. If we sleep-walk down to the gate, they'll cut us to bits."

+ + +

A bleary-eyed Fool Wolf made his way back down into the valley with dawn. Even under the circumstances, he found it beautiful. Mountains supported the heavens on all sides, raw-edged black stone clad where possible with spider bamboo, giant ferns, broad leafed evergreens and peculiar trees that looked like troops of green monkeys clinging to poles, their furry tails curling out to form foliage. Higher, ice ruled, the tallest peaks shrouded in swirling clouds. The valley was steep-walled and very green. Cattle and goats cropped in meadows, and fields of buckwheat ruffled in a light breeze. At the far end of the valley Fool Wolf could see the great gate; carved from the living mountain and flanked by towering monkey-faced giants of the same stone. Before it was the huge plaza where he had spent his day with the dead. Around the plaza was only meadow — no shrines or buildings, not even the little slate-roofed cottages that stood here and there in the valley.

Off to his right, two Nholish leagues distant and nestled into a narrow side valley, the golden towers of Nah glimmered fitfully in scattered shafts of sunlight. Behind the spires, mist obscured the mountains, so the Nah looked like the memory of a city, floating in a dream.

Fool Wolf turned toward the Nah, hoping it was only the plaza of the gate where strangers were slain on sight. It did not take him long to run across four soldiers, clad in fringed black kilts and henna-stained leather cuirasses. They carried spears and short swords dangled from broad belts. Their faces were generally very dark and lean, crowned with hair variously black, cream, and rust-colored.

"Stop there, stranger," one of them commanded.

"If it pleases you," Fool Wolf replied.

"What business have you in Nah?"

"I'm just a traveler, a trader of sorts," Fool Wolf told him.

"I see no pack animals, no goods. What do you trade?"

"Words. Things I've heard and know."

The soldier scrunched his brow. "This is a bad time for strangers. We've had tragedy here."

"Really? I'm sorry to hear that. Doubly sorry if it keeps me from earning a meal. A friend of mine told me I might find rest here."

"What friend was that?"

"He called himself Uzhdon, the Opal of Nah. We traveled together, for a time."

Their spears dipped toward him. "That is not a name to be said lightly," the oldest-looking of the men said, "Especially these days."

"Why is that? I assure you Uzhdon and I are friends. Take me to him, if you doubt me."

The man pursed his lips. "The Opal is not here. But I think the Rector might wish to see you, if you know anything of Uzhdon's travels."

"I was with him in Rumq Qaj, where we toppled the towers of blood, and in Pethvang, where the priests of the Sea cursed us for ending their evil rule." He did not mention that Uzhdon had been at least as interested in killing Fool Wolf on both occasions, or that he was still not clear on what the word 'evil' meant.

"Cursed?" One of the men blurted. "The Opal? That might explain —"

"Quiet, Limup," the eldest snapped. "Yes, stranger, I think the Rector would like a word with you."

"Has harm come to Uzhdon?" Fool Wolf asked, voice dripping with concern. "Nothing could bring me greater pain."

"Just come along. The Rector will explain what he pleases to you."

"Am I a prisoner?"

"Why find out?" the warrior replied. "Do as we say, and the question of your freedom will not have to be asked."

"Very well, then," Fool Wolf said. "I endeavor to be an honest man. Take me to your Rector, and I will speak. Knowing Uzhdon as I do, he would never ask me to lie or hold back."

"That's Uzhdon," the man allowed.

"What's your name?" Fool Wolf asked.

"Hoshut," the warrior replied.

And so they took him further down the road, through the gates of Nah, which he noticed were only leafed in gold — it was flaked, here and there, and he could see the stone beneath. That was something of a disappointment. Still, as the sun cut through the mist, the buildings caught the light and gilded it, rendering the very air lambent and precious. And Fool Wolf mused, if I scraped all of the gold from a building or two . . . .

But he had more pressing matters to consider.

Not everything was gilt, of course. Street vendors hawked wares from perfectly ordinary stalls, and the rambling houses at the edges of the city were stone, with copper or slate roofs. And the temple, the single largest building in the city, was remarkably plain, built of a grainy gray marble, shaped something like a gigantic wedge with the sharpest part pointed at the sky.

Within was mostly space, and priests chanting, burning incenses, pouring over scrolls and books. Tall statues held up the ceiling; the bodies of men and women with the heads of beasts — dogs, mostly, and wolves, and for a moment Fool Wolf stopped in his tracks, remembering the unearthly hounds and the terrible, usually faceless master of his dreams and visions.

"Magnificent, isn't it?" Hoshut said. "It still awes me, though I've served here often. There is no finer house for the gods anywhere, eh? Have you seen better, in all your travels?"

"No," Fool Wolf replied. He did not add that he thought anyone who made houses for gods at all had too much time on their hands and no sense of proportion. Gods lived in everything — they were everywhere. In Fool Wolf's experience, building houses for them either spoiled them or drove them mad, neither of which condition was desirable in a god.

Someone across the room caught his eye. A woman, seated on a bench, surrounded by children. She seemed to be speaking to them. Fool Wolf felt a weird little flutter in his chest, for he recognized her.

"Beautiful, isn't she?" Hoshut remarked. "She is the lady She'de'ng, recently come here from the faraway city of Nhol. She is a princess, there, but has come here to learn and study with our priests."

"Shouldn't we go?" Fool Wolf said. It would not do at all for She'de'ng to see him. When last he had met her, she and her lover, the sorcerer Lepp Gaz, had sworn to cut Chugaachik out of his chest, and Fool Wolf's heart along with the goddess. If She'de'ng was here, Lepp Gaz was, too, for the sorcerer's soul was in She'de'ng's keeping, and he would not let her roam far. He wondered what the odds were of being able to reach She'de'ng and kill her — and thus Gaz — and still escape the temple.

Not very good, he decided. It was stupid to cast three bones when the game required a hand of four.

"Life gets better each day," he muttered, under his breath, in his own language. If all of his enemies were fingers, they were closing into a fist and Fool Wolf in the palm. What was happening here?

"What was that?" Hoshut asked.

"A prayer, in my native tongue," Fool Wolf replied. "Surrounded by such holiness, I was overcome."

She'de'ng hadn't looked up yet, but she would. Fool Wolf tried not to fidget.

"Understandable," Hoshut said. "This way."

Hoshut took him into a labyrinth of smaller rooms, and at last to a plainly furnished one, having as it did only three small wooden stools.

"Wait," the warrior told him.

A moment later, Fool Wolf found himself alone in a securely locked room.

Carnivore scents padded behind Fool Wolf's eyes, and he tasted something bitter at the back of his throat.

"Hello, Chuugachik," he told his goddess.

That was a clever plan, she said. Walk up to the nearest warrior and ask to be taken prisoner. I wonder how long it will take Lepp Gaz to find us.

"I didn't know he was here!" Fool Wolf protested.

"Maybe he isn't. Maybe She'de'ng came here on her own."

She carries Gaz's soul tattooed on her flesh. Do you really think he would let her wander far from him?

"No. But She'de'ng didn't see us. If things work out as I planned, and I speak to the Lord Rector, he need never know we were here."

Another silent, mocking laugh. Unless Lepp Gaz is the Lord Rector. Certainly he is the one who called us all here.

"I'd thought of that," Fool Wolf reluctantly admitted. "The warriors in the plaza did say something about the Rector's foreign travels."

It would fit his nature, Chuugachik said. But — if we can kill Gaz, we can end this.

"You're sure it's him summoning you?

Isn't it obvious? Gaz covets me. He wants to add me
to the collection of souls tattooed upon his skin.

"It's more than that," Fool Wolf said. "When we first
met, he knew you, and you knew him. From where? From
when? How can he be powerful enough to control you?"

Chuugachik was silent for so long that Fool Wolf
decided she wasn't going to answer. He began searching
the cell for possible escape routes.

He is my brother, she said, finally.

"Your what?"

I thought he died long ago. I hoped he had. Now we
must kill him. I think it is our only chance. If we see
She'de'ng again, you must let me have your limbs.

"We'll see," Fool Wolf replied. "If Gaz is the Lord Rector,
we'll never get that chance."

At that moment, a small slot in the door opened, and
a pair of eyes appeared. Brown eyes, nearly black. Fool Wolf
felt his blood go to ice.

"Well? Who do we have here?"

"My name is Lohar Pang, of Fanva," Fool Wolf lied. "Are
you the Rector?"

"I am. You may address me as 'eminence'."

"Yes, eminence." One or two knots untied in Fool Wolf's
gut. Lepp Gaz had very pale eyes, not dark ones. And his
voice was different. Of course he might be able to change
his eyes, and his voice. Some sorcerers could do that.

"You traveled with Uzhdon, I'm told," the Rector said.

"Yes, eminence. For more than a year."

"And in that time did he behave — unusually?"

"He is the most perfectly virtuous man I have ever
know." That wasn't a compliment, to Fool Wolf, but it was
the truth.

"Of course. He is the Opal of Nah. But the warrior who
brought you here mentioned a curse . . ."

"Yes. The priests in Pethvang cursed Uzhdon. At first,
I thought they had failed, but then Uzhdon grew distant.
He woke often from sleep, and I found him wandering,
his eyes still dreaming. And then, one day, he and my other
companion — a woman named Inah — simply left me. That
wasn't like them, so I followed."

"I see. Can you tell me more of the nature of this curse?"

"No. Has Uzhdon . . . is he well?"

"He is anything but well," Rector grunted. "He has stolen the Heroq-priesthood key and opened the gate to the Strictured Land. It could well be the doom of the world."

"Why? What is this Strictured Land?"

"It was once the holiest of all lands, a land of plenty. Now it is a waste, and forbidden by the great gods. The First Evil sleeps there, and the Hounds of Ash. If Uzhdon wakes them, the mountains will not hold them in. They will reap humanity like grain."

"How do you know this?"

"The heart of the Strictured land was Xotar, the Living God. The Living One awoke to Evil, and his people with him. They were an affront to the gods of sky and mountain; The Seven-Bearded Hawk fell on them with his claws of lightning and the Snake of the Fourth Thunderbolt cut him with his jagged teeth. Those In Xotar who fought back were cursed and died with their city. Those who never succumbed to the spell of malice were led here. Then the mountains were thrown up and the way sealed. We are the chosen, the loyal. We guard the Strictured Land, and our heroes seek out the seeds of evil that scattered on the black winds when Xotar fell. Because we alone were spared, we cannot — must not — renege on our obligations."

"How do you know this?" Fool Wolf repeated.

"Because it is true," the Rector said, a bit sharply.

"Oh. In that case, you must know Uzhdon is the foe of Evil. He would never release it."

Fool Wolf was still a little shaky on what "evil" was, exactly, but he knew from experience that Uzhdon was not in favor of it.

"Not normally, no," the Rector allowed. "Our trust, these last five thousand years, has been to allow no one to open the gate. The Opal is our best, the most perfect example of what we are. If he has gone mad . . . " the Rector didn't finish the sentence.

"I'm sure this curse can't last forever," Fool Wolf said, soothingly. "Perhaps when Ilupor arrives —"

"What did you say?" The Rector snapped. Fool Wolf thought he sensed a bit of panic in his tone.

"Ilupor, Uzhdon's brother. We were to meet him here, tomorrow. He's coming on the west road."

The eyes blinked several times. "I see," the Rector murmured.

Then the eyes were gone, the slit closed again.

✛ ✛ ✛

Not much later, the door opened once more, and Hoshut stood there. He had a small package in his hands.

"This is for you," he said. "It is a gold bar, payment for your service to our temple. You will be provisioned and given a mount. Then I am to escort you from the valley."

"Must I go?"

The warrior nodded, and his voice dropped very low. "The offer is more generous than you know. If you stay, it will be as a corpse."

"But Uzhdon —"

"Is no longer your concern," the warrior replied. "We are his people. The Rector knows best, and Uzhdon would agree. If you know him, you know that."

✛ ✛ ✛

Fool Wolf regarded Hoshut, where he sat strapped to a tree.

"Not too tight, I hope?" Fool Wolf asked, mildly.

"You will regret this," Hoshut predicted.

"I would have regretted it much more if I had let you kill me," Fool Wolf said, reasonably.

"It is my duty to obey the Rector. His orders were to take you from the city and slay you quietly."

"Well, your duty has only got you tied up, rather than dead. I wouldn't complain, if I were you." Fool Wolf smiled and patted the fellow on the cheek. "Someone will happen by. Let's hope it's a kind-hearted soul."

"May you rot in the belly of Ghep."

"I'm only taking the deal you offered me," Fool Wolf replied. "And I notice, with amusement, that Uzhdon's people are not nearly so virtuous as he."

"There is only one Opal," the warrior replied, glumly, his head suddenly sagging. "and now he is lost to us. Perhaps it has made the Rector extreme. I do not question my orders, but I am glad I did not manage to kill you. It would have been dishonorable."

Fool Wolf rolled his eyes. "My greatest concern is your honor," he said. "So I'll leave you here, where there is no danger of you losing it."

As he walked off, he wondered if it was something in the water or the soil of Nah which bred such lunatics.

Fool Wolf peeked over the edge of the outcropping. He had a good view, both of the five men coming up the road from the west, and of the fifteen or so hidden on the hills overlooking the road, preparing to ambush the smaller party.

It was a nice place for an ambush, and the Rector's men were taking full advantage if it, with seven men on one side of the road and eight on the other. When the newcomers were in their crossfire, they would have nowhere to hide and little chance of scaling the steep embankments before being nicely punctured. So spare was the stony ground that only a few weeds grew, much too small to hide behind.

Fool Wolf waited until the newcomers were almost — but not quite — in range of their deaths, and then hollered at the top of his lungs, "Beware, Ilupor! Treachery!."

In more-or-less the same breath, he stood and shot the ambusher nearest him. The shaft struck the Rector's man in the upper chest, as he turned to see who had given them away.

Fool Wolf ducked as two red-fletched missiles sang through the rocks near him. The rest of the ambushers fired at the approaching quintet.

But too early. The range was too great, and all of the shafts fell wide. The group on the road split into two parties, three going right, two left. They scrambled up the banks — they were lower, there — and quickly found cover in the folded ridges of volcanic stone.

Fool Wolf had to duck, then — another arrow cracked on a rock a few handspans from him. He raised his bow to kill the archer as he fixed another arrow to his bow — and suddenly another attacker was there, leaping from behind Fool Wolf's ridge, curved sword cutting a slice of the sun.

Fool Wolf turned and fired, missed, and threw himself back as the blade whistled toward him.

The only sword Fool Wolf had was the one he had taken from Hoshut. It was curved, too, short and heavy. A cleaver, not a sword.

The ground gave him a good hard kick in the butt. It hurt, but he managed to roll behind another outcrop and take a few breaths. The warrior with the sword did not appear immediately, doubtless coming cautiously over the outcrop for fear of being shot. The Rector's man was in no danger of that, for the bow lay on the ground, too far away to risk running for.

Instead, Fool Wolf quickly pulled and arrow from his quiver and stuck it against his chest, as if his heart was pierced. He slumped against a rock, holding it there, and waited, eyes open and blank, tongue lolling out.

A moment later, the swordsman came around the rock and grunted in surprise. He'd been moving with prudent care, but now his back straightened, and he walked toward Fool Wolf with confidence. Fool Wolf tried not to blink or breath.

The fellow poked him with the tip of his sword. It hurt, but Fool Wolf didn't react. Satisfied, the man stepped in for a better swing.

Fool Wolf chopped his blade around and cut the warrior's left leg half-way in two at the knee. While the fellow was still trying to take that in, Fool Wolf stood, grabbed him by the collar, and split his head down the center.

He was just finishing that when someone else came around the corner, blade flashing. Fortunately, his first opponent was in the way of the blow, and the now-corpse had another huge gash in it. Fool Wolf wrenched his blade out and got it up in time to parry the next shot at his head. A third man, also in the Rector's livery, came over the hill to Fool Wolf's right.

He backed up quickly, knowing he couldn't go far, because there was a ravine somewhere behind him.

And then a fourth man leapt over the ridge, whooping a war-cry. His skin was dark umber, his hair a coppery red, and he bore a sword in each hand.

"Traitors!" He shouted. "Malefactors!"

Both of Fool Wolf's attackers turned at the sound, so Fool Wolf took that opportunity to chop the weapon hand off of the nearest. The man with two swords dispatched his opponent almost as quickly, then whirled on Fool Wolf. His eyes narrowed, then seemed to reflect vast surprise at something.

"You're the one who warned us!" The man with two swords said. Fool Wolf noticed he had curling lines tattooed on his forehead, just as he remembered Uzhdon having.

"I am," Fool Wolf panted.

"You're a brave man. We shall talk in a moment, when all of our cowardly foes are dealt with." With that he bounded off again.

Fool Wolf collected himself, then his bow, and followed.

✢ ✢ ✢

A short time later, Fool Wolf stood on the road with the man and his three surviving companions — one of their number had taken and arrow in the eye.

"There were fifteen," Fool Wolf told the man with two swords. "I watched them hide in the rocks."

"Well, we've killed them all, then. Thank you, stranger. Ilupor of Nah is in your debt."

"I am a hundred times in debt to your brother, Uzhdon,"
Fool Wolf replied. "I could not allow this base treachery
of the Rector to succeed."

"You know Uzhdon?"

"Indeed. We are the fastest of friends and companions."

"I am even more pleased to meet you, then. And so tell
me — is it true? Did the Opal of Nah really enter the
Strictured Land?"

"He did," Fool Wolf replied.

"Then he must have had good reason," Ilupor reasoned,
firmly. "Whatever he is up to, the Rector must not be
allowed to stop him. More, I must follow him into the
Strictured Land, and aid him in whatever task he has
set for himself. I am certain it is a noble one."

"My feelings exactly," Fool Wolf replied. "I know nothing about this Strictured Land of yours, but I trust Uzhdon's
judgment. I would aid him as well."

Ilupor clapped him on the back. "Say no more. You need
not prove yourself to me again. We have lost a companion, and the sacred texts say five is the luckiest number.
With you, we will be five again." He lifted his chin. "The
Rector sought to bar me from consulting the Sipost priests
who have the second key. He failed. Let us go see what
the Sipost priests have to tell us."

"The Rector sent these men to kill you," Fool Wolf
reminded him. "Why won't he send more?"

"Notice how few he sent," Ilupor said. "And that the
attack took place here, far from town and the sacred precincts. My guess is he sent only those men he trusted
absolutely, men with more loyalty than conscience — and
these were all of them. The rest he fears might be loyal to
Uzhdon — and thus to me." He scratched his head. "I
wonder how he even knew I was coming, or which road
I was coming by? I deliberately came by the least likely
way."

"Traitors aren't hard to find, I fear, even in fabled Nah,"
Fool Wolf bemoaned, wagging his head dolefully.

✛ ✛ ✛

By the time they reached the great temple, they had gathered a huge crowd. Many of these were armed, and some wore the livery of the Rector. More wore hawk feathers in their hair, and tattoos across their eyebrows.

"You see? Ilupor said. "The Rector dares nothing, here."

He swept confidently up the steps of the church, then paused, and turned to his crowd.

"Some say my brother Uzhdon has gone mad. I do not believe it, and neither do most of you. The sacred sword, Hukop, would never serve a madman, and yet from what I hear, he carries it still. For five thousand years, we have guarded the entrance to the Strictured Land, from whence our ancestors fled. For that long we have lived here, in constant risk our souls will be devoured by the void. No one doubts that the First Evil beyond those mountains is terrible; no one doubts that its slumbering power is awful. We have born the brunt of it for lo these generations.

"I believe Uzhdon learned of a way to end the evil, to destroy the threat of the Strictured Land forever. I believe the Lord Rector tried to kill him for that — after all, what use the Rector of a priesthood dedicated to guarding against a great evil if that evil is destroyed?"

That sent an angry mumbling around the crowd.

"And when I came, to take up my brother's task, to humbly request the second key to the gate from the Sipost priesthood, the Rector tried to slay me. He fears their decision!"

That drew a darker quality of growls and shouts.

"Now I go to receive that decision," Ilupor concluded. He turned to Fool Wolf. "My friend, would you do me the honor of guarding my back?

"I would indeed," Fool Wolf replied.

✚ ✚ ✚

Fool Wolf waited in the vast hall of the temple while Ilupor went into the sanctum of the Sipost priesthood. Two of Ilupor's followers stood with him.

Clever, Sweet thing. Chuugachik murmured, inside the chambers of Fool Wolf's heart. Now Ilupor will take you through the gate, assuming he gets the key. That was your aim, yes? To earn his trust?

"Yes," Fool Wolf mumbled.

And assuming that he's right, and the Rector can't summon enough men to slay him. And assuming he doesn't learn that it was you who betrayed him.

"There's no prize if the dice don't fall," Fool Wolf replied.

But you're forgetting Lepp Gaz. Find the woman, destroy his soul, and our troubles will be over.

"I somehow doubt that," Fool Wolf said.

"Stand there, Lady," one of Ilupor's men commanded, staring past Fool Wolf. "We do not know you."

"One of you does," said a familiar voice.

Fool Wolf felt suddenly very tired. He felt as if he had been treading a very narrow ledge and at last found its end. He turned to regard the Lady She'de'ng of Nhol.

"What an interesting reunion this is," she said, in the language of Nhol. "Hello, Fool Wolf."

"Lady She'de'ng," he said.

"Oh. You do remember me. How flattering. Do you remember everyone you betray?"

Fool Wolf couldn't repress an acerbic laugh. "You knew I would betray you. You counted on it, Lady, and you are not the innocent you pretended to be. In the end, I helped you get what you wanted, and to repay me you would have taken my life and let Lepp Gaz have my soul."

She shrugged. "If you remember it that way."

"And where is Lepp Gaz? Surely he would not let you stray far from him."

Her eyes fell. "I would not have thought so, and yet he did. Some sorcery is at work here. Something stronger than me or Gaz."

"So you say."

Her frown deepened. "Why are you here, Fool Wolf?"

"Why are you here, Princess?"

She tossed head back like an arrogant mare. "I was summoned," she said. "By dreams so irresistible that each night I took to walking from my quarters. Gaz could do nothing to stop them, so at last he outfitted an expedition to find the source of the summoning."

"And the summoning brought you here?"

"Yes. But our expedition was destroyed by barbarians across the mountains. I survived, and was discovered by a merchant bound for this place. He brought me here."

"And you think Gaz was killed? Fool Wolf asked.

"You know he was not. You know he cannot be, so long as I live, and his soul survives, tattooed on my flesh." She brushed her left breast, self-consciously.

"Then where is he?"

I don't know. Perhaps some beast ravages his body each time he heals it. Perhaps he is trapped beneath the waters of the river he fell in. I only know that in almost a moon, he hasn't found me."

"And the summoning?"

"I asked the Rector to keep me locked in my rooms, and he does so. I told him I am cursed, which must be the truth." Her eyes hardened. "Now I've told you why I came here. You owe me the same."

"I came hoping to steal some of the gold from these buildings," Fool Wolf said.

She looked skeptical. "But instead you've decided to help some local warrior in his holy struggle against the Rector?"

"I grew bored."

"That's nonsense. What do you take me for? You were summoned here, too, weren't you? You've also had the dreams of the hounds, the great city, the terror. I'm sure this hero of theirs, this Uzhdon, had the same dreams. Something beyond those mountains wants us. All of us."

"I am sorry, princess, but I've no idea what you mean."

Anger contracted her cold face into a scowl. "Why lie to me? We must be allies in this. A common enemy afflicts us."

"Princess, I'll remind you once more — last time I sought to help you, it nearly ended in my death, and you would have been pleased. Do not plead with me."

"I —" but she turned to stare.

Ilupor had just staggered from the doorway to the Sipost precincts. He was bleeding heavily from a cut to his forearm.

"Blasphemy!" He moaned. "The priests were all dead, and assassins in their place! The key was gone! The Rector has broken the sacred laws!"

"Ilupor, you are wounded!" One of his men cried.

"It is an ant-bite," the warrior said. "I must speak to the people. When they hear — when they see what the Lord Rector has done, they will know it is not my brother who is mad, but he."

✛ ✛ ✛

Ilupor had four hundred men with him by the time they reached the plaza of the gate. The Rector's men were waiting, in nearly even numbers. The two leaders faced each other across a space no greater than a weak man might throw a stone.

"You have sinned," Rector," Ilupor shouted. "All here know it. You took the Opal of Nah prisoner, then you tried to kill him. You tried to kill me, too, in cowardly ambush, and you did slay the Sipost priests when they would not give you the key — the key you need to pursue and slay Uzhdon."

"This is madness!" The Rector shouted back. "Our sole purpose is to keep anyone — even our own Opal — from treading the sands of the Strictured Lands. Don't you fools know your Tesoths? 'When the living tread the shattered bricks of Xotar, then grins the first Evil and wakes.' What matter that it is Uzhdon?"

"What matter? And yet you would go there."

"Wait!" The Rector held up is hands. "A moment! First, I did not slay the Sipost priests, or cause them to be slain! I, like you, courted their favor, and I think they were disposed to give it to me."

"You lie!" Ilupor said.

"I do not! Furthermore, my only aim in entering the Strictured lands is to stop Uzhdon before it is to late."

"I trust my brother before I trust you! The Opal of Nah is righteous, while you have proven yourself a sinner. Give us the key!"

"If I had the key, wouldn't I have already gone through the gate?"

"This is some sort of trick!"

The men around Fool Wolf were at fever pitch. He could actually smell their fury and fear.

When did you steal the key and murder the priests? Chugaachik asked. Clever, but I don't remember.

"It wasn't me," Fool Wolf replied, pursing his lips tightly.

Then who?

Fool Wolf shook his head. "I don't know."

The Rector's eyes suddenly lit on Fool Wolf, and recognition flashed there. That couldn't be good.

Fool Wolf launched himself at Ilupor.

"Watch out!" he shouted. "A murderer's arrow!"

Ilupor went down under Fool Wolf's weight, but before they even hit the stone, the mob was in motion, sweeping toward the Rector's men like a tide. No one seemed interested in whether some hidden sniper had actually tried to kill Ilupor or not; in a heartbeat all reason was gone from the field.

Ilupor bounced up. "Once again I owe you my life, friend," he shouted. "Come, fight by my side!"

This was the messy part of Fool Wolf's plan, and he hated it. He despised fighting. He especially loathed pitched battles, where cleverness, agility, and skill were poor shields against the chaos of death all around. He might normally slink off or pretend to be wounded, but in this case he had to take the risk. He had to go through that gate with Ilupor. Ilupor had to trust him, and he would only trust a warrior.

So he fought, and hated it, and was happy that it was over soon. The Rector's men collapsed under the assault, and the Rector himself fell with an arrow in his throat. More than half of Ilupor's mob died, as well, and before the sun set again, the plaza of the gate was as Fool Wolf had first found it — a corpse garden.

But in that tumult and confusion, Fool Wolf did see something interesting. He saw Ilupor stoop over the dying Rector, and Ilupor had a dull green something in his hand. He pushed his hand into the Rector's robes and brought it out empty. Then he drove his right-hand sword straight into the Rector's heart.

Later, Ilupor produced the key to the gate from the Rector's dead body, before all of the survivors of the battle.

It was jade, a little larger than a man's palm, and Fool Wolf wasn't surprised.

Nodding to himself, Fool Wolf slipped off, hoping that in the hysteria the Temple and the Heroq-rite shrine had been left unguarded.

✛ ✛ ✛

"Ah, there you are!" Ilupor said. "Where have you been all night?"

"Cleansing myself," Fool Wolf replied. "It's a custom of my people, after battle — to avoid the sickness that vengeful ghosts can bring."

"Ah. You must tell me more of this custom, some day. But didn't you sleep?"

"I did not."

"Are you fit to travel with us?"

"I am."

And so, a bit later that morning, Ilupor opened the gate with the key of Jade.

The expedition consisted of Ilupor and thirty warriors, Fool Wolf — and She'de'ng.

"She is a foreign princess, somehow cursed by the Strictured Land," Ilupor confided. "The Rector was keeping her prisoner."

"But should we take her with us?" Fool Wolf asked. "Won't it be dangerous for her?"

Ilupor considered, stroking his chin. "It is all part of some puzzle," he said. "My brother, this princess, the insanity of the Rector. She's willing to go, and I think we should take her."

Fool Wolf shrugged. "It's your expedition. Do you know what we will find?"

"A long tunnel through the dark. Many traps, to stop the unwary." He paused. "There is a problem, there. Uzhdon seems to have taken the Heroq-rite book detailing the various pitfalls in the tunnels. We must brave them even so."

"I am ready for that," Fool Wolf assured him.

✠ ✠ ✠

The light of day died behind them, and soon they had only the fire goddess to guide the way. They advanced cautiously, for what seemed a very long time, until at last they reached a narrow stone bridge, spanning what might as well be a bottomless cavern.

"That looks like a good place for a trap," Fool Wolf observed.

"Indeed it does," Ilupor agreed. "A trap that can survive five thousand years could not rely on trip-cords and such. It's mechanisms must be all of stone, or worked by some little god."

"Let me cross first," Fool Wolf said. "I am acquainted with this sort of thing."

"That's generous, but this is not your fight," Ilupor replied. "One of my men will try it."

"Uzhdon is my friend," Fool Wolf insisted. "I insist that the honor be mine."

"Do you?" Ilupor said, a suspicious note in his voice. Fool Wolf wasn't looking at him, but he heard the faint wisping of a sword coming free from its scabbard.

Fool Wolf ran, as swiftly as his feet would take him. As he set foot on the stone bridge, an arrow hissed by his ear, but he set his mouth and kept running, eyes down, counting stones by torchlight. When his foot hit the fourteenth stone, he felt it sag and click. He threw the torch ahead and leapt with all of his might.

The bridge groaned and fell to pieces, and he hit the far lip of the ravine with one foot. He tottered there a moment, until the impact of an arrow striking his shoulder gave him the final nudge to fall forward and not back. He closed his teeth on the pain, and rolled for cover.

"Stop firing!" Ilupor commanded. "He has the book! He must have taken it from the Heroq-rite shrine."

Fool Wolf groped for the arrow and found it wasn't there — it had struck his scapula and rebounded. "That's very well reasoned," he shot back, in the language of Nhol. "Well reasoned indeed, Lepp Gaz."

That echoed in the ravine for a moment, followed a moment later by She'de'ng's mocking laughter.

"When did you know?" Gaz replied, still in Ilupor's voice.

"Always," Fool Wolf said. That wasn't true — he hadn't known until he saw "Ilupor" secret the key upon the Rector.

"You're very clever, then. My disguise fooled even his own men. I have Ilupor's soul, after all, and thus all he knew."

"What are you up to, Gaz? What is waiting for us in the Strictured Land?"

"Everything. You're an idiot to fight me, Fool Wolf. We should be allies."

"I'll judge that for myself, when I know more," Fool Wolf told him.

"Give me the book. I can still forgive you."

"How generous," Fool Wolf said. "But I don't have it anyway. I couldn't read it, after all, though the illustrations were clear enough. I memorized the drawings and burned it." He darted forward and snatched up the torch. His wound, however shallow, was really starting to hurt. It wouldn't do to faint here.

"Good luck with the rest of your journey," Fool Wolf shouted back. "The bridge-trap was just the first of many. There are much more inventive snares ahead."

Ignoring the sorcerer's howl of frustration, Fool Wolf turned and hurried down the tunnel, deeper — toward the Strictured Land.

I think you have doomed us both, Chuugachik murmured, in the deep of his bones.

"I was doomed the moment I took you as my spirit helper," Fool Wolf told the goddess. "If I'm to die, I'm only to happy to take you with me."

He continued through the darkness, ignoring the goddess' curses.

HOUNDS
OF
ASH

The Hounds of Ash
Part Three

WHEN THE ASHES CAME TO LIFE, Fool Wolf knew that the fever from the wound in his shoulder had finally reached his head. Or it might have been the dehydration, or both. Whatever the case, it was a bad sign.

He had to admit, however, that the hallucinations improved things in some ways. For two days he had trudged the table-flat plains of the Strictured Land, his feet sinking to the ankles in gray-black dust so fine that even the motion of his feet surrounded him with a cloud of it. Now his nostrils and lips were crusted with soot, he coughed up black mucus, and boulders of grit gathered in the corners of his eyes. In the day the sun beat him like a blacksmith's hammer, and at night his breath smoked from the cold. The wound in his shoulder pulsed blood and pus, and his waterskin was almost empty.

Still, if nothing else, his new madness broke the monotony. His fever lifted the ash like fog, congealing it into the forms of trees, boulders, rushes, flowers and grass. A road appeared beneath his feet, hard and level. It formed, like the trees, a stone's cast ahead of him and dissolved the same distance behind and to each side. Birds clotted into being, flitted to the edge of his insanity, and decayed into plumes of dust.

The trees offered some shade from the sun, at least. He would have been happier if the landscape had some color in it, rather than the same uniform charcoal hue as the plain, but Fool Wolf had a long list of rather-nots that took precedence over the quality of his fever-dreams. He would rather not be in this forsaken place, for instance, he would rather not be wounded, he would rather he wasn't being pursued by perhaps the most powerful sorcerer in the world.

Interesting, murmured the goddess who made her home within Fool Wolf's bones. The goddess, of course, was his greatest rather-not of all, because without her, none of the others would exist.

Fool Wolf ignored the comment. Chugaachik's interests ran toward torture, perversion and violent murder, all of which she used Fool Wolf's body to accomplish whenever he was foolish or desperate enough to invoke her power. If she found something 'interesting' it was better not to know what she meant.

Instead, he sat down on a small shelf of stone that had assembled itself from the ash, scooted until he was beneath the shade of an unreal date palm, and drew out his waterskin. There were two mouthfuls of water in it, and he took one, letting it remain in his mouth for a while, trickling it only slowly down his throat.

Ebony cattails waved in a breeze, and a coal-colored heron waded in a dark simulacrum of water. He dipped his hand into the 'stream' and brought up only ash. He managed a sardonic laugh.

It's not fever, you know, Chugaachik said. What you see is real.

"Is it?"

I see it, and your fever doesn't affect me.

"What's doing it? Gods? Ghosts?"

We haven't passed near a god since we entered the Strictured Land.

That was unusual, in and of itself. The world teemed with gods. Every stream, tree, forest, stone and hilltop had at least a minor god in residence. The great gods — those who claimed to have created the world itself — were more removed, living in the sky, the highest mountains, the deepest forests, far from Human Beings.

"None?" he asked.

None.

"Then what is this?" He waved at the monocolor phantoms around him.

I don't know.

"You seem to know very little these days. Are you ready to tell me what is drawing us onward, or where we are going?"

The same sorcery that compelled us here clouds my memory, the goddess answered. As well you know.

"I wish I could tell when you are lying." Fool Wolf sighed and stood shakily. The summoning had first affected him only in sleep, but now he could feel a sort of lodestone in his head, pointing the direction but growing red-hot if he rested too long.

I do know we must reach our destination before Lepp Gaz. Chugaachik offered.

"Why?"

I don't know.

Fool Wolf rolled his eyes in disgust. "Well, since I left him sealed in the mountain behind us, we have a chance of that, at least. What about Uzhdon and Inah? They're probably there already."

Mentioning Inah brought a hard twang of emotion he had come to expect, though he still didn't understand it. The daughter of the Python King was beautiful, of course, and his memory of her bare, brown curves and smoky green eyes aroused him even now, but he had had many lovers. And Inah could be cruel — she had tried to starve him to death when they first met. And she had abandoned him to his death in the city of Pethvang in order to travel with Uzhdon, a man who had tried to kill Fool Wolf on several occasions.

Still, he missed her.

He started off again, brushing his way through the colorless and frangible leaves of tamarisk, olive, and fernpear trees.

At sundown, monsters reared from the dust, twin lions with the heads of jackals. With their paws folded beneath them, their heads towered as high as twelve men. The sight struck steel to flint inside of Fool Wolf's skull, igniting a vision he had had before only in the depths of sleep.

✛ ✛ ✛

His feet touched upon gray stone, a plain that stretched away to jagged peaks in very direction. Two of them exhaled plumes of dark ash. He walked, and after a time came to a city of the same stone. Flanking the broad way were twin statues, crouching figures of jackal-headed lions beside which Fool Wolf was ant-sized. Their eyes gleamed like fishscales, and the sight of them brought blood to his loins and jolted a fierce anger through him. He laughed, Chugaachik's laugh.

Beyond the statues, the city was massive cubes and columns, and a thousand thousand kneeling men and women in rags. They seemed to be chanting a hymn as gray dust from the sky settled on their shoulders.

And something parted the crowd in the distance, a man in the mask of a black-beaked bird. A darkly patterned kilt his only clothing, his flesh was so white it seemed to shine. The crowd shouted a name to him, but Fool Wolf could not make it out. The masked man came on, white light blazing through the eyeholes of his mask, until he stood directly in front of Fool Wolf.

In one hand the masked figure held the leashes of four hounds, or what Fool Wolf first took for hounds. One was as white as his master, so gaunt as to be almost skeletal, with sapphire eyes. The next was more tiger than dog, hunch-shouldered like the grass bears of Fool Wolf's native steppes. The third, sleek and gray, had the head of a hawk, and the fourth was a black, squirming mass that might have been made of worms.

Now Fool Wolf wanted to run, but his feet were rooted. The Earth began to tremble, and the hounds drew so near the stench of their breath made him want to vomit.

The masked figure halted, regarded him for a long moment, then removed his mask.

The face was so magnificent Fool Wolf wanted to weep, and he feared the beauty was so terrible he would die from the mere sight of it. But then the face changed, and became the dark, narrow, high-cheekboned face of a Mang. Fool Wolf's face.

These were the statues. This was the valley. But on the
plain before him, not even a brick stood to suggest a city
had ever been there.

Fool Wolf caught a motion from the corner of his eye,
just in time. Something large, gray, and four-legged raced
toward him, leaping even as he turned. Fool Wolf dropped
and rolled on his shoulder and was nearly blinded by
appalling pain — he'd rolled onto the shoulder one of Lepp
Gaz's men had impaled with an arrow. A grotesque howl
he hardly recognized as his own tore from his throat, but
he managed to draw the cleaver-like sword he had stolen
in the city of Nah.

The creature was still for an instant, facing him. Aside
from the fact that it was the same gray-black as everything
else in the valley — right down to its eyes — it was the
emaciated hound from his vision.

That's a very dangerous thing, Chugaachik informed
him.

"Is it a god?"

I've never seen anything like it. But it will kill you unless
you call on my strength.

"No."

Look around you. You fear the little games I play when
you free me, I know. But who shall I play them on here?

Fool Wolf raised his sword. "Inah is here somewhere.
You'll find her if I let you."

She betrayed you, fool! She left you to drown and went
with your enemy, Uzhdon. What do you care about her?

"That's my affair," Fool Wolf replied, about the same
time that the creature lept at him.

He held his ground till the last instant, then dodged
aside, dropping a decapitating blow to the monster's neck.
Braced for a shock, Fool Wolf was surprised when all he
felt was a thin, gritty resistance. The blade followed through
into the ground.

The creature snarled, pawed at him, then ran back off
across the plain. Fool Wolf watched it go, breathing deeply,
gripping his aching arm.

"Not so dangerous after all," he commented.

It will be, in time, Chugaachik promised.

"How do you know?"

When Chugaachik didn't answer after twenty breaths, Fool Wolf shrugged and looked around. The beast, whatever it was, had collapsed into dust by then.

"That's the first time you've bade me invoke you since this whole mess began," he noticed. "In fact, you spent two months cowering as deep in my bones as you could burrow without even whispering to me, something you've never done since I was cursed with you. Now all of a sudden — since we entered the Strictured Land — you've become your old self again. What's changed?"

Invoking me gives the summoning more power over us. It was prudent to avoid that, during the journey. But the summoning is over. We're here, now. We've reached the place we were called to.

She was right, Fool Wolf realized. The lodestone in his head no longer pointed anywhere.

I didn't want to come here, she continued. I do not like being enspelled, because few are powerful enough to do it. Very few, and they are very dangerous. Even Lepp Gaz did not have that power of old, but he has found it now. But you've brought us here, and now our only choice is to fight and win. I'm ready to fight again. Prudence was never much fun.

"Fine," Fool Wolf said, though he was certain she still wasn't telling him everything. "If this is the end of our trail, Uzhdon and Inah ought to be here, too," he reasoned.

He noticed he was on a high point in the plain — a gentle rise, unnoticeable from a distance, scarcely noticeable even when standing on it. Perhaps where he stood had been a plaza or something similar — someplace without trees or high features, for no apparitions stood in the way of his view. He could see the whole plateau, all the way to the mountains.

Back the way he had come he noticed the faintest plume of dust. Nearer, only half a league of so away, he saw a little oasis of shadow trees.

"There you are," he muttered, and started toward the oasis.

✤ ✤ ✤

As Fool Wolf's phantasmic landscape merged with that of the oasis, he found himself confronting a ridiculously large sword — a sword colored sword, wielded by a large, dark-skinned man with auburn hair and curling tattoos over his eyebrows. The eyebrows were presently raised in an expression of extreme surprise.

"Hello, Uzhdon, Opal of Nah," Fool Wolf said.

In reply, the sword rose a bit higher, presumably for better chopping. Despite its almost comical size, Uzhdon wielded it like a switch.

"Remember your promise," Fool Wolf said. "You aren't supposed to kill me until we're done with this."

"Are you really Fool Wolf?" Uzhdon asked, "or just another of these smoke spirits?"

"What color am I, Uzhdon?" Fool Wolf asked.

The warrior grunted. "You aren't the same as the rest, I agree, but — I left you . . ."

"You left me to drown. I don't blame you for being surprised to see me, but it is me."

Uzhdon lowered his weapon slowly.

"Fool Wolf!" Inah appeared from behind a tree. "You finally made it!"

She was just as he remembered, golden-skinned, lithe, with hair like midnight. She threw herself into his arms, and in an instant his head was full of her faintly snaky scent. The feel of her flesh against his was shockingly good.

He pushed her back to arm's length. "You could be more surprised," he said. "You left me to die, too."

"Not a violation of our agreement," Uzhdon sheepishly pointed out.

"I was aware of that at the time," Fool Wolf told him. "I expected you to leave me." He looked Inah full in the eyes, something his people did only when they were delivering an insult. "I guessed you would leave me, too."

Inah flashed her pearly teeth. "I knew you would survive — you always manage to float to the surface."

"I knew you would leave me," Fool Wolf went on, "by the way you were looking at Uzhdon. What I don't know is exactly why."

Inah glanced at Uzhdon. "Fool Wolf and I will walk for a bit," she told the warrior. "Alone."

"Inah, he is evil," Uzhdon warned.

"There you go with that word again," Inah replied. "Come on, Fool." She tugged at his hand.

They walked through what seemed to be a well-tended garden on paths through weaving topiaries and rock formations, along canals full of lilies, past stelae spidered in strange characters.

"Well?" Fool Wolf broke the silence.

"Uzhdon keeps trying to explain this word "evil" to me," Inah said. "I don't really understand."

"I don't either. Except that whatever evil is, apparently I am it."

"Yes, he's mentioned that before, too."

"That's Uzhdon. He's always either standing still or galloping, nothing in between. There's no doubt in him. You aren't like that, though. Are you going to tell me why you left me to die, after all I've done for you?"

"Shall we count how many times I saved your life?" Inah asked. "If we score it, I don't think you will come out ahead." She leaned close. "Besides, shouldn't we let our muscles get reacquainted, before more of this tiresome talking? Uzhdon talks all the time." She looked him up and down. "There's that shoulder, but I'm sure we could work around that."

That was a pretty powerful temptation, even in his state of near dehydration, but Fool Wolf shook his head. "Why are you here?" he demanded.

She chewed her lip petulantly, then shrugged. "At first I was in this because you were. I was curious to discover what was making you walk at night. Then we met Uzhdon, and it was clear the two of you had been drawn together."

"And then both drawn here."

"Yes. But when I saw Uzhdon, I suddenly felt the pull, too. I started having visions and then nightmares about a man in a bird mask, with four beasts —"

"I know the vision," Fool Wolf said.

"Uzhdon was going to leave you, no matter what I did, and I somehow didn't think it was wise to let him go off on his own. He isn't like you or me, you know." She smiled again. "Besides, Pethvang was coming apart. I knew your goddess would see you through, and I knew you would follow us. I figured I could keep an eye on Uzhdon until then."

"I'm happy you had faith in me."

"Fool Wolf, don't pretend you wouldn't have done the same. I know you that well, at least. What did you think, that I wanted that oaf for a mate?"

"I —"

"He's not a very inventive lover."

Fool Wolf tasted the implications of that and didn't like them very much. He didn't say so — instead he put on his best stranger-in-the-girl's tent smile and said, "Well no, of course not, not compared to me. Don't you know I'm the best lover that ever lived?"

"You were my first, how could I know that?"

Hoping Uzhdon was within shouting distance, Fool Wolf reached for her. "Well, let me remind you, then. Watch the shoulder."

☩ ☩ ☩

"And so this Leep Gas is following you?" Uzhdon said, later.

Fool Wolf swallowed another mouthful of water before answering. Uzhdon had plenty of water, and at Inah's insistence was sharing it.

"Lepp Gaz," he corrected. "He's a sorcerer. He steals souls and tattoos them on his body. They give him the strength and power of his victims. His own soul he keeps elsewhere."

"An evil sorcerer, then," Uzhdon reasoned. "When he gets here, I shall slay him."

"Be my guest," Fool Wolf replied. "If you think you can do it. It won't be easy, though." He paused for another drink. "I think it's Gaz who called us to this place." And Chugaachik claims Lepp Gaz is her brother. And despite her power, even she fears him, he almost finished. But he couldn't think why he should tell Uzhdon that.

"Aha. Your sorcerer means to awake the First Evil," Uzhdon asserted. He poked a blunt, callused finger at Fool Wolf. "I suspect you do, too. The evil god you keep in your body was drawn here by the Evil."

"I see," Fool Wolf replied, happier than ever that he hadn't confirmed the link between Chugaachik and Lepp Gaz. "You were drawn here too. Are you therefore evil?"

Uzhdon looked surprised, like a child who has just heard the last thing he expected to hear. "I bear Hukop," he explained, "my godsword. My totem is the Seven Bearded Hawk, who defeated the First Evil ages ago. Naturally we have been called to defeat him once again."

"And Inah? Why was she summoned here?"

"To aid me. She has a powerful spirit in her as well."

"Yes. She's half god, the daughter of the Tattooed Python King. But why do you think she's here to help you?"

"The Seven-Bearded Hawk was assisted in destroying the Evil by Mehas, the Snake of the Fourth Thunderbolt. I believe her soul is that of Mehas, at least in part."

"I see. And so how will Lepp Gaz — who is, by the way, as much my enemy as you are — how are the two of us going to awake this First Evil? And for that matter, where is it?"

"I don't know, but be assured I won't give you the chance. I will slay the sorcerer, and if you attempt anything sinister, I shall slay you as well, despite my oath. You've tricked me with your honorless ways before. You won't do so again. Better I break my vow and suffer personal dishonor than see the whole world under the heel of the First Evil."

"Why would he put the whole world under his heel?"

"Because he's evil," Uzhdon said. "He tried once before."

"According to your legends."

"According to the holy and uncorrupted facts of the matter my people have passed down for generations. And to Hukop."

"Well, I see I can't argue with you," Fool Wolf said.

"Because you know I'm right," Uzhdon said.

"No," Fool Wolf said, scratching his cheek, "for the same reason I wouldn't argue with a pile of dog dung."

"No need to be unfriendly," Uzhdon replied, his eyes widening.

"Weren't you just talking about killing me?"

"Only if it becomes necessary, and then without malice or ill will," Uzhdon explained, his voice betraying a bit of hurt.

"Well, that will be a great comfort," Fool Wolf said. "Meantime, could we discuss a plan? Lepp Gaz will be here soon."

"So you say. If it's true, it's no matter — none can slay me in other than a fair fight while I carry Hukop."

"Lepp Gaz has an impressive sword, as well," Fool Wolf said. "Yours is bigger, but his has more sting. And he has no soul in his body — I've seen him cut nearly in half and survive."

"Besides," Inah put in, "just because you can't be killed doesn't mean we can't."

"That's true," Uzhdon said. "Let me do all of the fighting, then. I wouldn't want you hurt."

"He has a lot of men with him," Fool Wolf said. "He disguised himself as your brother, Ilupor, and has some of his followers."

"He what?" Uzhdon bolted up to his full height, eyes flashing. "What became of my brother?"

"I suspect he is tattooed on the sorcerer's skin. As I said, that's how Gaz gets his power."

Uzhdon trembled with rage, and tears squeezed from his eyes. "I shall —" he stopped, suddenly, and his eyes narrowed. "Is this one of your tricks? Are you trying to trick me into slaying my own brother? Fool Wolf, I warn you —"

He broke off as a beast suddenly erupted from the foliage. At first Fool Wolf thought it was the same creature which had attacked him earlier, but as it leapt over Inah and onto Uzhdon, he saw that it was one of the other hounds from the vision, the sleek one with the head of a hawk.

It also seemed much more substantial than Fool Wolf's attacker, for its claws savaged great gashes in the warrior's shoulders. Impressively, the Uzhdon kept his feet during the first rush, and more impressively, managed to hurl the beast off of him. In an instant, he had Hukop poised over his head. He struck down, splitting the beast in half.

It didn't stay in two halves, however. Color poured into it like oil across sunlit water, and as it thus shimmered, it came back together. Now it appeared exactly as it had in Fool Wolf's visions — sleek and gray, but an altogether different shade from the all-pervading ash. Its eyes flashing with unmistakable glee, it turned and ran off across the plain, as Uzhdon sank to his knees, a wail of inconsolable grief tearing from his throat. Hukop dropped from his hands.

Fool Wolf continued to watch the hawk-headed beast. It did not vanish when it reached the limits of the unreal landscape, but continued loping back in the direction Lepp Gaz was coming from.

"Uzhdon?" Inah knelt beside the big man. "Uzhdon, are you well? What's the matter?"

Uzhdon turned a blood and ash-streaked face toward them, his eyes wide and uncomprehending.

"Hukop is gone," he murmured.

"Your sword is right there," Inah soothed.

"It's only metal, now," Uzhdon groaned. "My totem is gone. The Seven-Bearded Hawk is gone."

"Horse Mother," Fool Wolf swore. At the edge of the trees, the other beast — the one which had attacked him earlier — appeared and vanished, appeared again, stalking the circumference of the spectral gardens. Another of the vision-monsters was with it — the wormy mass that only resembled a dog or cat in the vaguest way.

"We have to get out of here," Fool Wolf said. "Now."

Uzhdon shook his head as if clearing water from his ears, then came to his feet. He lifted his sword with obvious effort. Without the god in it, it must have been incredibly heavy. "Take Inah," He murmured. "I stand and fight."

"I'm very impressed by that plan," Fool Wolf said. "Come on, Inah."

"Wait. Where? Where can we run? What if they just run around him and follow us? Then we'll just be one fewer when they catch us."

"We're already fewer," Fool Wolf whispered in her ear. "Look at him trying to hold that sword."

Let me deal with them. Chugaachik said. I can kill all of them — the beasts, Lepp Gaz, his warriors. I can end this now.

"End what now, Chugaachik?" Fool Wolf asked the goddess, softly. "What's happening?"

He didn't get an answer, and the gaunt beast suddenly bounded toward him, just as the other lurched toward Inah.

Fool Wolf whipped his sword out and ran straight at his attacker. At the last moment he suddenly changed direction, flinging himself toward the hound attacking Inah. He buried the edge of his weapon in it's skull, wrenched it out, and hacked again, into the thick neck. It was like chopping into a bag of sand. The beast reared up and swiped at him with a massive paw. Fool wolf ducked and cut at the neck from underneath. The head burst into a cloud of ash. The body held together for a moment longer, then collapsed.

He spun, wondering why the other beast hadn't hit him yet, and saw Uzhdon had it from behind in a wrestler's hold, arms locked under its paws. The warrior's arms bulged with effort. Abruptly, the whole beast collapsed. Overbalanced, Uzhdon tumbled to the ground.

They will be back, Chugaachik told Fool Wolf. Stronger.

"We have to move," Fool Wolf said. "Find a better place to fight these things."

Inah caught his arm with her fingers and clamped there. It hurt. "I am not without power, Fool Wolf. You know that. Why did you turn your back on the beast attacking you to battle mine?"

"Inah, you saw what happened to Uzhdon."

"So? You've fought two of these things, now, and nothing happened to you."

"That's right. Because I have an ordinary hunk of metal to start with." He waved the heavy blade around. "No god in this. Nothing for them to steal."

"I don't even have a weapon — oh!"

"Yes. What happens if they steal the half of you that is a god? Do you want to find out?"

She pursed her lips. "Maybe it doesn't work that way. After all, you have a goddess in you —"

" — and if I invoked her, I would probably lose her."

Inah tilted her head and placed her fists on her hips. "Isn't that what you want? To be rid of her curse?"

"Yes. But not if she gets a body. Isn't that right, Chugaachik?"

You have no idea what you're talking about, sweet one. Uzhdon's sword was a special thing.

"Those beasts were the hounds of ash," Uzhdon said. "They were the servants of the First Evil. They herald his return."

"But what did the hound do to Hukop?" Inah asked.

Uzhdon grimaced. "Devoured him, I think. These phantoms need sustenance, the lifeblood of gods, to give them true form. When they all have form, they will summon the First Evil."

"Do your sacred texts say that?" Fool Wolf asked.

Uzhdon bit his lip. "Not exactly. But it makes sense, doesn't it?"

Fool Wolf hid an amazed expression. "Anyway," he said, "we should move."

"Again, to where?" Inah asked.

Fool Wolf gestured back toward the higher ground. "Over there. There aren't any trees or gardens or such. We can at least see them coming."

"And when Lepp Gaz gets here?"

Fool Wolf shrugged. "We can always try running — back through the tunnels and out of this valley. Maybe now that we've come here, the compulsion is over with, and we can leave."

"Coward!" Uzhdon declared.

"No," Inah said. "I tried that already. The pain comes back, worse than before."

Fool Wolf nodded. "Very well. Uzhdon and I fight these things off while we wait for Lepp Gaz. Then we'll see."

"Then I'll kill him," Uzhdon promised. He began walking in the direction Fool Wolf indicated, dragging his massive sword behind him.

✣ ✣ ✣

They fended off three more attacks by the beasts, each more vicious than the last. When Lepp Gaz arrived, Fool Wolf and Uzhdon were smeared with their own blood.

Gaz halted fifty paces away. He was still in the guise of Ilupor, Uzhdon's brother. The two weren't twins, but they looked very much alike, with their fine dark features and reddish hair. Behind Gaz were ten warriors with umber kilts and hawk feathers in their hair. Next the sorcerer stood a dark, willowy beauty — the princess She'de'ng, from the far away city of Nhol. It was through her that Fool Wolf first met the sorcerer, when she hired Fool Wolf to assassinate him. Now she wore his soul on her skin, making him effectively immortal. Of course, Fool Wolf knew that particular secret, so he was a bit surprised to see She'de'ng in such an exposed position. If he could manage to destroy the tattoo on her, Gaz would die.

Or would he, in this place?

The bird-headed hound was with them, too, as were the two that had been attacking Fool Wolf and Uzhdon, along with the final beast — the massive, hunch-shouldered one — still as gray as ash.

"Brother? Is that you?" Uzhdon called.

"Don't be an idiot," Fool Wolf said.

"Of course it is me," Gaz said. "Who else would I be? I've come to help you destroy the First Evil, brother."

Uzhdon's lip trembled. "Fool Wolf claims you are a foreign sorcerer."

"Fool Wolf is an honorless liar, as I'm sure you know," Ilupor said. "He pretended to be your friend — our friend — slaughtered the Sipost priesthood and stole the key to the gate into this place."

Uzhdon met the sorcerer's gaze. "What was the name of the dog we had as children?" he asked.

"Uzhdon," Fool Wolf said, "he has all of the knowledge your brother had."

"His name was Klenop, of course, a small black-and- and tan hunting dog."

Uzhdon nodded.

"Uzhdon —" Fool Wolf began.

"You aren't my brother," Uzhdon said, flatly. "That was the name of our dog, but we were just children when we gave it that name, and didn't know better. It's an obscene term, one my brother would no longer speak. You have stolen my brother's memories, but have none of his character. I will kill you."

Some of the men behind Gaz looked confused. Others looked as if things made sense for the first time.

"You men are fighting for evil, for a man who would resurrect the First Evil," Uzhdon said. "You are my men. You belong at my side."

One of them, an older man with copious tattoos, knelt in the ash. "We cannot, Opal of Nah. This man we thought your brother has taken our souls. We cannot do what he does not allow." He looked defiantly at the sorcerer. "But we need not obey him, either."

"No you need not," Lepp Gaz said, and with that each of the men dropped limp and lifeless to the ground.

"Now," he said, stepping forward. "It's time to finish this."

Kill him, Chugaachik urged. Kill him now, or it is the end of us both.

Lepp Gaz stepped forward, raising his hand.

The dust swirled and then lifted as if in a mighty sand-storm. From across the plain it came, hissing against flesh, blinding him. Fool Wolf shut his eyes tightly. He sum-moned up the godsight which Chugaachik gave him without him having to invoke her, but it was equally confusing — the air seemed full of the glowing heartstrands that signified life and puissance. After an instant, he could stand no more and relinquished the supernatural vision.

After a time, the wind died, and in its place, the city of
Xotar stood, or the ghost of Xotar, sculpted of ash. It's
towers and monoliths rose like the spires of mountains,
and its gate — just behind them — could have admitted
a whale such as he and Inah had spied in the waters near
her home. Huge terraced pyramids surrounded the vast
plaza they all stood on.

Gaz smiled, and drew a slim, black blade. He started
forward, and so did the two beasts which had been attacking them.

Uzhdon braced himself.

"No," Fool Wolf said. "Not here. Into the city."

"He killed my brother."

"Then you'll want to actually defeat him, rather than
die a stupid death," Fool Wolf snapped. "Come on!"

"Listen to him, Uzhdon," Inah said. "He's been right
so far."

Uzhdon's lips compressed and then turned down, but
he nodded curtly.

Fool Wolf didn't wait another second, but turned and
ran through the massive gate.

But he turned at Inah's shriek. She had stumbled, and
Fool Wolf saw blood on her thigh. The hounds were almost
on her, Lepp Gaz and She'de'ng strolling confidently
behind. Lepp Gaz was carrying what resembled a blowpipe.

Inah's eyes blazed like green lightning, and she suddenly bounced up, darting forward with incredible speed,
charging Lepp Gaz. Just before she hit him, she elongated
and became a snake with scintillating green and yellow
scales.

She never reached him. The amorphous hound bounded
into her and locked its jaws on her torso. She turned and
clamped it in her mouth.

The hound took on color, and the snake dissolved. Inah's
limp, naked form fell motionless to the ground.

And Lepp Gaz laughed.

Uzhdon roared inarticulately, but Fool Wolf gripped his
arm.

"We'll avenge her, I promise. But not here!"

Uzhdon stood there, rigid for a moment, and then the two of them ran into the city.

✠ ✠ ✠

They ran through halls that could have held palaces and plazas the size of towns. They passed gargantuan statues of the god in the hawk mask and strange basins for which Fool wolf could see no purpose at all. And still they ran, until they reached a point where the walls were less substantial, fuzzier.

"Where are we going! We must turn and fight!"

"No!" Fool Wolf puffed out. He didn't have the breath to explain, and frankly didn't care, except that he needed the thick-headed warrior. "Keep — go — faster!"

Soon they were running in a duststorm, like the one that precipitated the city and then, finally, they broke into clear air. Fool Wolf dropped to the ground, panting, Uzhdon beside him.

As they watched, the walls built themselves, and the city was finally whole.

✠ ✠ ✠

"How did you know the city hadn't finished forming on this side?"

"I'm all knowing," Fool Wolf told him.

"No, really."

"It was a small guess based on a larger guess," Fool Wolf replied. "I was right about one, so I'm nearly certain I was right about the other."

"I don't understand."

"Never mind. Let me explain a few things instead, about Lepp Gaz."

"You said he was a soul stealer."

"Yes. That sword of his — if he stabs someone with it, it takes his soul and distills it into a black fluid. Lepp Gaz then has the fluid tattooed on him. He can keep the bodies alive that way — after all, a body can't be killed if its soul survives."

"Then my brother is still alive? And Inah?"

"Probably. That's why I was trying not to get you killed. Saving them is better than avenging them, don't you think?"

Uzhdon looked surprised. "That's very kind of you. I — owe you an apology. I thought you were part of this plot to bring back the First Evil. It now seems clear you are not."

Fool Wolf shrugged that off. "Its not important. Here is what is: Lepp Gaz keeps his own soul out of his body, as well. But he also keeps it near him, where he can protect it. Last I knew, his soul was on the body of She'de'ng."

"But she can't die. You just said so."

"True. But if a blade or a spear happens to pass through the tattoo which holds his soul, it will be released."

"Ah! And then he can die."

"Yes."

"But why would he risk her, so, if that's the case?"

"Maybe he's too confident of his own power. Anyway, it doesn't matter. What does matter is that it's our only chance. And you're the one to do it."

"Strike an unarmed woman?"

"You don't have to kill her. I'll explain where the tattoo is. You can use my sword. And remember — she can't die."

"I still don't like it."

"Do you want to save your brother, Inah, and the world from the First Evil?"

"Yes."

"Then you'll have to trust me."

Uzhdon looked skeptical. "I've trusted you before, and paid a dear price."

"Yes, and in Pethvang I not only freed you from a terrible fate, I was repaid for that by being left to suffer the same fate I rescued you from. I'd say we were even."

Uzhdon colored slightly. "I'm not proud of that," he said.

"Exactly. Cutting She'de'ng won't make you proud, either, but it's what you have to do. What was that you said earlier, about personal dishonor being preferable to letting the First Evil walk?"

Uzhdon smiled grimly. "I can hardly deny my own words," he replied. "How do we do this?"

"They'll be looking for us in the city. Hopefully they won't expect us to come in behind them. First, though, we're going to need some of your water."

"I'm thirsty, too."

"Not to drink."

✛ ✛ ✛

When they reentered Xotar, they were the same color as its walls, painted with a mixture of water and ash. They slipped down its silent streets, alert for signs of the enemy.

"Help me find them, Chugaachik."

You will have to summon me to survive.

"Just help me find them."

The walls suddenly vanished, as Fool Wolf's vision nudged into the otherworld. Or, rather, they ceased to be walls, and became instead tapestries of living heartstrands.

The city obscures them.

"At least Gaz suffers from the same handicap," Fool Wolf said.

"Here," Uzhdon said. "Their feet leave faint marks in the ash."

Fool Wolf squinted, and indeed, saw faint scuff marks on the simulacrum of stone.

"Good eyes," he said. "we'll —"

Uzhdon tapped him on the shoulder and pointed. One of the hounds stood only a stone's throw away, staring in their direction. It's nose pricked up.

Hide us from it, Chugaachik.

It's alone, sweet thing. What better chance have we to kill it?

"Hide us from it," he repeated.

I can't.

And I know you can.

Anger boiled in Fool Wolf, not his own. The beast looked up, sniffed again, and continued on into another hall.

The two men followed the trail through half a league of city and into a vast room supported by pillars in the form

of twining snakes. Within, Fool Wolf heard the faint echo
of voices — She'de'ng and Lepp Gaz speaking.

They crept closer, from pillar to pillar, until they were
only a small distance away.

Fool Wolf glanced around his hiding place. Lepp Gaz
sat cross-legged on a large cube incised completely around
with some sort of angular writing. She'de'ng rested on a
slightly lower throne, and the two hounds which had been
given color crouched at their feet. Inah lay limply between
the beasts, her eyes wide and unseeing, but her breast rising
and falling with breath.

"Now?" Uzhdon whispered.

"Wait. Wait until I say."

"I can hear you, you know," Lepp said, in a dreamy
voice. "You might as will step out so I can see you, too."

"I don't believe we will," Fool Wolf replied.

"You can both live through this," Lepp Gaz said, reasonably. "There is no need for either of you to die."

Fool Wolf's teeth suddenly hurt and a powerful craving
to taste blood swept through him. His heart palpitated with
excitement, and for a moment he thought he would faint.
Images flashed through his head — a disemboweled Lepp
Gaz, Lepp Gaz with no eyelids, Lepp Gaz with the skin
of his palms cut off. The smell of urine and cedar.

"No!" Fool Wolf muttered. "Stop it, Chugaachik. Lady
She'de'ng! Don't you know how he will use you?"

"Poor Fool Wolf," she replied, in her lilting, aristocratic
accent. "You don't know me at all, do you? I know exactly
what my portion will be."

"When the First Evil returns, your portion will be only
death!" Uzhdon bellowed.

Lepp Gaz laughed. "The First Evil is a children's story
you idiots in Nah have been telling yourselves for five
thousand years. Don't you know the truth, yet? Are you
so dense, Opal of Nah?"

"I was entrusted with Hukop, the guardian. I know the
truth! I know what you would resurrect!"

"Hukop lost his mind because of what we did," Lepp
Gaz said. "He deluded himself, and then your people.
Children."

Fool Wolf noticed a movement from the corner of his eye. It was the skeletal hound, bearing down on him silently, jowls open.

"Now, Uzhdon!" Fool Wolf cried. "Now, Chugaachik!" And he opened himself to the goddess.

His vision jolted red and green-black, and scent smote him — the stinging alkaline of the ash, Uzhdon's sweat, She'de'ng's faint jasmine perfume, the scratchy musk of Inah. And the hound, the hound filled his vision, and he sank his talons into it gleefully as it cut into him, and he was glad, overjoyed, and with a more than sexual intensity, gratified in a burst of pleasure so powerful it knocked him writhing to the ground. And Chugaachik's laughter, all around him, in him but seeping out, tearing from the throat of a hound now become real.

And then Chugaachik was no longer in Fool Wolf. He was empty of her.

"Finally! Finally!" the beast shrieked, shivering like a heat mirage. "Fool Wolf, my sweet, you have no idea what you have done."

Fool Wolf clambered to his feet. "Wrong," he said. He turned and ran as fast as he could toward the others.

Uzhdon stood over the collapsed form of She'de'ng, waving a bloody sword and turning on Lepp Gaz. Gaz stood, a laugh frozen on his lips, as the final hound filled with the rainbow. Fool Wolf could feel Chugaachik's breath just behind him, as he leapt forward, snatching the black sword from Lepp Gaz's frozen hand. Then claws like glass ripped into his back, and he watched in dull surprise as blood speckled the floor he was tripping toward, a floor which was swirling with color, like the walls, the columns, the roof, as Xotar became real.

But he twisted as he fell, and the point of the sword went through the neck of the newest hound, the hound that was really Lepp Gaz, and its eyes went wide and a terrible howl broke from its throat before it fell back into dust. The pain in Fool Wolf's back vanished almost as swiftly, and he rolled back to his feet. The hound that was Chugaachik stopped short, staring at the point of the weapon with sapphire eyes.

Then the hound uncoiled like a snake, rose high and twisted together, and became a woman with ebony skin and eyes of green fire, beautiful, perfect, stunningly desirable.

"Sweet thing," she murmured, in a voice that promised everything. "we've been together for so long. What are you doing?"

"Stopping you," he said.

"Give me that sword, or you'll force me to kill you."

"We'll see about that."

Chugaachik showed a mouthful of white needles. "You actually did me a favor," she said, swaying toward him. "Lepp Gaz might have been the one to choose our incarnation, but now that falls to me. Which means I can give you your every wish, my sweet. You can be our consort." She waved at Uzhdon and the insensible Inah. "We can keep them as pets, if you wish."

"I don't understand!" Uzhdon wailed.

Chugaachik turned her gaze to the warrior. "Pitiful creature. Your precious Hukop is part of us, do you understand? Together we slew our father, and thus won our freedom."

"These four," Fool Wolf said. "They are your First Evil."

Chugaachik beamed. "We were among the first, brother to Balati the Forest Lord. We watched the great gods dream and lose form, decay into many smaller gods, and we swore it would never happen to us. We built a city and took for ourselves a people, and they worshipped us. Their worship held us together for millennia. But our father made us as aspects of himself, and that was his downfall. We plotted, destroyed him, and divided what remained of his power between us. We ruled this place as siblings until they day we too quarreled, and in the following war lost everything. Hukop became deranged, and deteriorated into what you knew him as — a deluded guardian, afraid of going forward, afraid of going back. Mehas went far away, and put his essence in a human vessel to make himself immune from the call, should it ever come. Lepp Gaz wandered as a sorcerer, remembering something of the glory and trying to recapture it. I was most cursed of all, unable to manifest form, doomed to serve pitiful shamans like you. You brought us all back together again Fool Wolf. This is your triumph, and you can share in it. Only release Lepp Gaz from that sword."

"I see no reason to do that," Fool Wolf replied.

"I am fond of you, sweet thing. You have helped us, after all." She waved at Uzhdon. "He is a fool, with his conceptions of good and evil. You know better. There is only power."

"Indeed," Fool Wolf replied. "Power I hesitate to give you."

Her voice dropped to a purr. "If you don't want to share, then you can be free, as easily as that. You are free of me already. Release Gaz and be on your way."

"I won't do that either."

"Three of us are incarnate. You can't stop us."

"I think I can," Fool Wolf replied. "I'm willing to bet that unless all four of you are incarnate you not only can't merge back together, you can't even leave this valley without losing your bodies again. You'll be stuck here forever, with no one to torture or murder. Maybe you'll even turn on each other once more."

He advanced a step, the sword pointed out at arm's length. "Or we can do this, instead."

Chugaachik narrowed her eyes. "Don't, sweet thing. You won't like the result."

For answer, Full Wolf thrust with all of the speed in his command.

Chugaachik fell to dust before the blade reached her. He felt a sudden wave of sickness as she returned to her home in his heart.

Is this what you wanted?

"It's the only way," he said.

The other hounds tried to run, but they reacted too slowly, and Fool Wolf was full of the strength and speed of the sword. He took them as he had taken Lepp Gaz, as around him Xotar collapsed once more into ash.

✛ ✛ ✛

Inah's remarkable eyes filled once again with intelli-
gence. She blinked up at Fool Wolf. Then slowly took in
her surroundings.

"Where are we? I don't remember."

"In Nah, in Uzhdon's house. How do you feel?"

"Tired."

"Disappointed?" Fool Wolf asked.

"I don't know what you mean. I remember attacking
the sorcerer, and then —" she shook her head. "It's confusing. I wanted something, I remember. Very badly."

Fool Wolf nodded and gripped her hand.

"Did we win?" She asked.

"That depends upon what you mean," Fool Wolf replied.
"Lepp Gaz failed, and so did Chugaachik. So did you."

He opened the front of the loose robe Uzhdon had given
him. Across his chest was scrolled a black tattoo, a snake
twisting back on itself.

"You used Gaz's sword," she said, her voice flat. "That's
my soul, isn't it?"

"It is."

"You could have put it on me."

"I don't think so. Lepp Gaz wasn't alone in his aspi-
rations. All of you conspired, didn't you? Chugaachik
didn't even know what was happening until she entered
the Strictured Land. But you did. You brought me and
Uzhdon together. It was never Lepp Gaz summoning us,
it was you. Gaz knew what was happening, and meant to
take advantage of it — but you started it."

Her eyes hardened, a bit. "I wasn't sure what I was
doing at first," she said. "When I met you I could feel the
possibilities — I could feel the other two, far away." She
sighed. "Don't you know what we could have done?"

Fool Wolf laughed. "Why would I care? Chugaachik was
a part of it — I wasn't. And you've been known to be —
shall I say careless? — with my life."

"We wouldn't have hurt you."

Fool Wolf leaned in and kissed her on the forehead. "I
don't trust anyone who even has that decision to make."

"Where are Gaz and Hukop?"

"In the sword, still. It wasn't easy to figure out how to get you out and not them, but I managed it. Even that was a risk I shouldn't have taken, but I did. And the sword — I suspect no one will see it until the world ends, if even then. Chugaachik, of course, is safe again with me. And if you're interested, She'de'ng and Uzhdon are both well."

She sat up. "And me? What becomes of me?"

He shrugged. "If Uzhdon ever discovers you knew what you were doing, I suspect one of the other of you will die. Me — well, I have your tattoo on my skin. Without Gaz's sword to extract it, my fate is your fate. You can't kill me without killing yourself, not unless I return to the Strictured Land. Which I won't. I'll die first." He smiled. "And that is that. There's plenty more to do in the world, Inah, then to become what you were five thousand years ago. After all, the four of you failed when you had everything in your grasp. You would have failed again, after a thousand years."

"But you might have shared those thousand years with us."

"Or you might have killed me like a flea."

She sighed. "I thought I liked you," she said.

"Yes, and I do like you. I just can't trust you."

"And so we part now?"

"Well, that's the most interesting question of all. Do I worry for the rest of my life that you're just behind the next rock, with some plot to kill me and steal your soul back, or do I keep you in my sight? Which would be safer for me?"

She smiled, a narrow, almost playful smile. "A choice I don't envy you. Which will you do?"

"I don't know. But either way, life will be more interesting."

Our titles are available at major book stores
and local independent resellers who support
Science Fiction and Fantasy readers like you.

EDGE Science Fiction
and Fantasy Publishing

Tesseract Books

Dragon Moon Press

www.edgewebsite.com
www.dragonmoonpress.com

Our titles are available at major book stores and local independent resellers who support Science Fiction and Fantasy readers like you.

Alien Deception by Tony Ruggiero -(tp) - ISBN-13: 978-1-896944-34-0
Alien Revelation by Tony Ruggiero (tp) - ISBN-13: 978-1-896944-34-8
Alphanauts by J. Brian Clarke (tp) - ISBN-13: 978-1-894063-14-2
Apparition Trail, The by Lisa Smedman (tp) - ISBN-13: 978-1-894063-22-7
As Fate Decrees by Denysé Bridger (tp) - ISBN-13: 978-1-894063-41-8

Billibub Baddings and The Case of the Singing Sword by Tee Morris (tp)
- ISBN-13: 978-1-896944-18-0
Black Chalice, The by Marie Jakober (hb) - ISBN-13: 978-1-894063-00-5
Blue Apes by Phyllis Gotlieb (pb) - ISBN-13: 978-1-895836-13-4
Blue Apes by Phyllis Gotlieb (hb) - ISBN-13: 978-1-895836-14-1

Chalice of Life, The by Anne Webb (tp) - ISBN-13: 978-1-896944-33-3
Chasing The Bard by Philippa Ballantine (tp) - ISBN-13: 978-1-896944-08-1
Children of Atwar, The by Heather Spears (pb) - ISBN-13: 978-0-88878-335-6
Clan of the Dung-Sniffers by Lee Danielle Hubbard (pb) - ISBN-13: 978-1-894063-05-0
Claus Effect, The by David Nickle & Karl Schroeder (pb) - ISBN-13: 978-1-895836-34-9
Claus Effect, The by David Nickle & Karl Schroeder (hb) - ISBN-13: 978-1-895836-35-6
Complete Guide to Writing Fantasy, The - Volume 1: Alchemy with Words
- edited by Darin Park and Tom Dullemond (tp)
- ISBN-13: 978-1-896944-09-8
Complete Guide to Writing Fantasy, The - Volume 2: Opus Magus
- edited by Tee Morris and Valerie Griswold-Ford (tp)
- ISBN-13: 978-1-896944-15-9
Complete Guide to Writing Fantasy, The - Volume 3: The Author's Grimoire
- edited by Valerie Griswold-Ford & Lai Zhao (tp)
- ISBN-13: 978-1-896944-38-8
Complete Guide to Writing Science Fiction, The - Volume 1: First Contact
- edited by Dave A. Law & Darin Park (tp)
- ISBN-13: 978-1-896944-39-5
Courtesan Prince, The by Lynda Williams (tp) - ISBN-13: 978-1-894063-28-9

Dark Earth Dreams by Candas Dorsey & Roger Deegan (comes with a CD)
- ISBN-13: 978-1-895836-05-9
Darkling Band, The by Jason Henderson (tp) - ISBN-13: 978-1-896944-36-4
Darkness of the God by Amber Hayward (tp) - ISBN-13: 978-1-894063-44-9
Darwin's Paradox by Nina Munteanu (tp) - ISBN-13: 978-1-896944-68-5
Daughter of Dragons by Kathleen Nelson - (tp) - ISBN-13: 978-1-896944-00-5
Determine Your Destiny #1: Petrified World by Piotr Brynczka (pb)
- ISBN-13: 978-1-894063-11-1
Distant Signals by Andrew Weiner (tp) - ISBN-13: 978-0-88878-284-7
Dominion by J. Y. T. Kennedy (tp) - ISBN-13: 978-1-896944-28-9
Dragon Reborn, The by Kathleen H. Nelson - (tp) - ISBN-13: 978-1-896944-05-0
Dragon's Fire, Wizard's Flame by Michael R. Mennenga (tp)
- ISBN-13: 978-1-896944-13-5
Dreams of an Unseen Planet by Teresa Plowright (tp) - ISBN-13: 978-0-88878-282-3

Dreams of the Sea by Élisabeth Vonarburg (tp) - ISBN-13: 978-1-895836-96-7
Dreams of the Sea by Élisabeth Vonarburg (hb) - ISBN-13: 978-1-895836-98-1

Eclipse by K. A. Bedford (tp) - ISBN-13: 978-1-894063-30-2
Even The Stones by Marie Jakober (tp) - ISBN-13: 978-1-894063-18-0

Fires of the Kindred by Robin Skelton (tp) - ISBN-13: 978-0-88878-271-7
Firestorm of Dragons edited by Michele Acker & Kirk Dougal (tp)
   - ISBN-13: 978-1-896944-80-7
Forbidden Cargo by Rebecca Rowe (tp) - ISBN-13: 978-1-894063-16-6

Game of Perfection, A by Élisabeth Vonarburg (tp)
   - ISBN-13: 978-1-894063-32-6
Green Music by Ursula Pflug (tp) - ISBN-13: 978-1-895836-75-2
Green Music by Ursula Pflug (hb) - ISBN-13: 978-1-895836-77-6
Gryphon Highlord, The by Connie Ward (tp) - ISBN-13: 978-1-896944-38-8

Healer, The by Amber Hayward (tp) - ISBN-13: 978-1-895836-89-9
Healer, The by Amber Hayward (hb) - ISBN-13: 978-1-895836-91-2
Hounds of Ash and other tales of Fool Wolf, The by Greg Keyes (pb)
   - ISBN-13: 978-1-894063-09-8
Human Thing, The by Kathleen H. Nelson - (hb) - ISBN-13: 978-1-896944-03-6
Hydrogen Steel by K. A. Bedford (tp) - ISBN-13: 978-1-894063-20-3

i-ROBOT Poetry by Jason Christie (tp) - ISBN-13: 978-1-894063-24-1

Jackal Bird by Michael Barley (pb) - ISBN-13: 978-1-895836-07-3
Jackal Bird by Michael Barley (hb) - ISBN-13: 978-1-895836-11-0
JEMMA7729 by Phoebe Wray (tp) - ISBN-13: 978-1-894063-40-1

Keaen by Till Noever (tp) - ISBN-13: 978-1-894063-08-1
Keeper's Child by Leslie Davis (tp) - ISBN-13: 978-1-894063-01-2

Lachlei by M. H. Bonham (tp) - ISBN-13: 978-1-896944-69-2
Land/Space edited by Candas Jane Dorsey and Judy McCrosky (tp)
   - ISBN-13: 978-1-895836-90-5
Land/Space edited by Candas Jane Dorsey and Judy McCrosky (hb)
   - ISBN-13: 978-1-895836-92-9
Legacy of Morevi by Tee Morris (tp) - ISBN-13: 978-1-896944-29-6
Legends of the Serai by J.C. Hall - (tp) - ISBN-13: 978-1-896944-04-3
Longevity Thesis by Jennifer Tahn (tp) - ISBN-13: 978-1-896944-37-1
Lyskarion: The Song of the Wind by J.A. Cullum (tp)
   - ISBN-13: 978-1-894063-02-9

Machine Sex and other stories by Candas Jane Dorsey (tp)
   - ISBN-13: 978-0-88878-278-6
Maërlande Chronicles, The by Élisabeth Vonarburg (pb)
   - ISBN-13: 978-0-88878-294-6
Magister's Mask, The by Deby Fredericks (tp) - ISBN-13: 978-1-896944-16-6
Moonfall by Heather Spears (pb) - ISBN-13: 978-0-88878-306-6
Morevi: The Chronicles of Rafe and Askana by Lisa Lee & Tee Morris
   - (tp) - ISBN-13: 978-1-896944-07-4

Not Your Father's Horseman by Valorie Griswold-Ford (tp)
 - ISBN-13: 978-1-896944-27-2

On Spec: The First Five Years edited by On Spec (pb)
 - ISBN-13: 978-1-895836-08-0
On Spec: The First Five Years edited by On Spec (hb)
 - ISBN-13: 978-1-895836-12-7
Operation: Immortal Servitude by Tony Ruggerio (tp)
 - ISBN-13: 978-1-896944-56-2
Operation: Save the Innocent by Tony Ruggerio (tp)
 - ISBN-13: 978-1-896944-60-9
Orbital Burn by K. A. Bedford (tp) - ISBN-13: 978-1-894063-10-4
Orbital Burn by K. A. Bedford (hb) - ISBN-13: 978-1-894063-12-8

Pallahaxi Tide by Michael Coney (pb) - ISBN-13: 978-0-88878-293-9
Passion Play by Sean Stewart (pb) - ISBN-13: 978-0-88878-314-1
Plague Saint by Rita Donovan, The (tp) - ISBN-13: 978-1-895836-28-8
Plague Saint by Rita Donovan, The (hb) - ISBN-13: 978-1-895836-29-5

Reluctant Voyagers by Élisabeth Vonarburg (pb) - ISBN-13: 978-1-895836-09-7
Reluctant Voyagers by Élisabeth Vonarburg (hb) - ISBN-13: 978-1-895836-15-8
Resisting Adonis by Timothy J. Anderson (tp) - ISBN-13: 978-1-895836-84-4
Resisting Adonis by Timothy J. Anderson (hb) - ISBN-13: 978-1-895836-83-7
Righteous Anger by Lynda Williams (tp) - ISBN-13: 897-1-894063-38-8

Shadebinder's Oath by Jeanette Cottrell - (tp) - ISBN-13: 978-1-896944-31-9
Silent City, The by Élisabeth Vonarburg (tp) - ISBN-13: 978-1-894063-07-4
Slow Engines of Time, The by Élisabeth Vonarburg (tp) - ISBN-13: 978-1-895836-30-1
Slow Engines of Time, The by Élisabeth Vonarburg (hb) - ISBN-13: 978-1-895836-31-8
Small Magics by Erik Buchanan (tp) - ISBN-13: 978-1-896944-38-8
Sojourn by Jana Oliver - (pb) - ISBN-13: 978-1-896944-30-2
Stealing Magic by Tanya Huff (tp) - ISBN-13: 978-1-894063-34-0
Strange Attractors by Tom Henighan (pb) - ISBN-13: 978-0-88878-312-7
Sword Masters by Selina Rosen (tp) - ISBN-13: 978-1-896944-65-4

Taming, The by Heather Spears (pb) - ISBN-13: 978-1-895836-23-3
Taming, The by Heather Spears (hb) - ISBN-13: 978-1-895836-24-0
Teacher's Guide to Dragon's Fire, Wizard's Flame by Unwin & Mennenga - (pb)
 - ISBN-13: 978-1-896944-19-7
Ten Monkeys, Ten Minutes by Peter Watts (tp) - ISBN-13: 978-1-895836-74-5
Ten Monkeys, Ten Minutes by Peter Watts (hb) - ISBN-13: 978-1-895836-76-9
Tesseracts 1 edited by Judith Merril (pb) - ISBN-13: 978-0-88878-279-3
Tesseracts 2 edited by Phyllis Gotlieb & Douglas Barbour (pb)
 - ISBN-13: 978-0-88878-270-0
Tesseracts 3 edited by Candas Jane Dorsey & Gerry Truscott (pb)
 - ISBN-13: 978-0-88878-290-8
Tesseracts 4 edited by Lorna Toolis & Michael Skeet (pb)
 - ISBN-13: 978-0-88878-322-6
Tesseracts 5 edited by Robert Runté & Yves Maynard (pb)
 - ISBN-13: 978-1-895836-25-7
Tesseracts 5 edited by Robert Runté & Yves Maynard (hb)
 - ISBN-13: 978-1-895836-26-4

Tesseracts 6 edited by Robert J. Sawyer & Carolyn Clink (pb)
- ISBN-13: 978-1-895836-32-5

Tesseracts 6 edited by Robert J. Sawyer & Carolyn Clink (hb)
- ISBN-13: 978-1-895836-33-2

Tesseracts 7 edited by Paula Johanson & Jean-Louis Trudel (tp)
- ISBN-13: 978-1-895836-58-5

Tesseracts 7 edited by Paula Johanson & Jean-Louis Trudel (hb)
- ISBN-13: 978-1-895836-59-2

Tesseracts 8 edited by John Clute & Candas Jane Dorsey (tp)
- ISBN-13: 978-1-895836-61-5

Tesseracts 8 edited by John Clute & Candas Jane Dorsey (hb)
- ISBN-13: 978-1-895836-62-2

Tesseracts Nine edited by Nalo Hopkinson and Geoff Ryman (tp)
- ISBN-13: 978-1-894063-26-5

Tesseracts Ten edited by Robert Charles Wilson and Edo van Belkom (tp)
- ISBN-13: 978-1-894063-36-4

Tesseracts Eleven edited by Cory Doctorow and Holly Phillips (tp)
- ISBN-13: 978-1-894063-03-6

Tesseracts Q edited by Élisabeth Vonarburg & Jane Brierley (pb)
- ISBN-13: 978-1-895836-21-9

Tesseracts Q edited by Élisabeth Vonarburg & Jane Brierley (hb)
- ISBN-13: 978-1-895836-22-6

Throne Price by Lynda Williams and Alison Sinclair (tp)
- ISBN-13: 978-1-894063-06-7

Too Many Princes by Deby Fredricks (tp) - ISBN-13: 978-1-896944-36-4

Twilight of the Fifth Sun by David Sakmyster - (tp)
- ISBN-13: 978-1-896944-01-02

Virtual Evil by Jana Oliver (tp) - ISBN-13: 978-1-896944-76-0

Greg Keyes

Greg Keyes was born in Meridian, Mississippi. He received degrees in anthropology from Mississippi State University and the University of Georgia before becoming a full-time writer. He is the author of the Star Wars 'New Jedi Order' novels, 'The Age of Unreason' and 'The Kingdoms of Thorn and Bone' tetralogy. He lives in Savannah, Georgia.